"You are behaving recklessly."

"You're right," Eleanor said, looking shocked. "You're right. I am behaving recklessly. And if I am going to behave recklessly, then it ought to be to get what I actually want." She laughed. "If I'm going to lose everything...I should really try to lose everything."

And before Hugh could ask what she meant, she drew closer to him, her scent intoxicating, and he remembered that scent from last night. The way he had taken her into his arms before cruelly rebuffing her.

And he had been cruel. More, he had been a liar. An outright liar. And she looked so beautiful in this dress. So innocent. Like everything she was. Young and pretty and forbidden. And he craved her.

And she wouldn't do it. She wouldn't close the distance between them, because she was too innocent. Because she didn't know how to do it. So it was up to him. Up to him to destroy all that he had built with one touch of his mouth to hers.

And in a breath, the decision was made.

MILLIE
ADAMS

—

The Duke's
Forbidden Ward

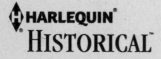

HARLEQUIN®
HISTORICAL™

Recycling programs
for this product may
not exist in your area.

ISBN-13: 978-1-335-40782-5

The Duke's Forbidden Ward

Copyright © 2022 by Millie Adams

Harlequin Enterprises ULC
22 Adelaide St. West, 41st Floor
Toronto, Ontario M5H 4E3, Canada
www.Harlequin.com

Printed in U.S.A.

Millie Adams has always loved books. She considers herself a mix of Anne Shirley (loquacious but charming and willing to break a slate over a boy's head if need be) and Charlotte Doyle (a lady at heart, but with the spirit to become a mutineer should the occasion arise). Millie lives in a small house on the edge of the woods, which she finds allows her to escape in the way she loves best—in the pages of a book. She loves intense alpha heroes and the women who dare to go toe-to-toe with them (or break a slate over their heads).

Books by Millie Adams

Harlequin Historical

Scandalous Society Brides

Claimed for the Highlander's Revenge
Marriage Deal with the Devilish Duke
The Duke's Forbidden Ward

Visit the Author Profile page
at Harlequin.com.

Chapter One

1818

If there was one thing Hugh Ashforth, the Duke of Kendal, would never tolerate, it was a scandal.

Eleanor Jennings knew that, as well as she knew anything. For she knew His Grace well. Privately she called him Hugh. Only to herself. When she lay down to sleep at night and she thought of him. Thought of what it might be like if he took her into his arms and danced with her.

If he took her into his arms and…

The very idea made her blush and she couldn't afford to be flushed. She was being trotted out at yet another ball at yet another country house party.

So far beneath all those in attendance, and yet bearing a great dowry courtesy of the Duke.

And there was the fact that she was beautiful. Uncommonly so, it was said, but Eleanor had not yet found that to be a boon.

No, instead she found herself continually fending off men who were greedy in all senses of the word.

And now with the Duke's sister, her best friend Beatrice, off and married, Eleanor did not even have someone she could complain about the evening with afterwards.

She loved Beatrice like she was her own sister. But she also felt some guilt because Hugh was giving her a season, while he'd been adamant against giving Bea one.

Due to concerns over her health, Hugh had determined that Bea shouldn't marry, for carrying a child could be too difficult for her. But then Bea had got herself ruined—in the arms of Hugh's best friend, and a terrible rake—and now she was off and married and Hugh had been…

Well, he'd been an absolute nightmare to cope with in the time since.

And she was without her friend.

'You look beautiful.' Her lady's maid finished arranging her hair, and Eleanor took a moment to look at herself in the mirror. But then her focus wandered to Hettie, her maid.

Eleanor's father had been a fairly successful merchant who'd had business dealings with the Duke, and they'd forged a friendship. When he'd taken ill her father had begged the Duke to take Eleanor on as his ward. And she knew that if Hugh were not beset by a near crippling sense of duty he would not have done so. Without his guardianship, she'd have been destined for a position as a housemaid. If she could have found herself such a fortunate position.

If not…

There were other options.

Beatrice was Eleanor's best friend. Though Eleanor was always conscious of the differences between them. One thing Eleanor loved about her was that Bea clearly did not see those differences. She was cloistered and protected from the realities of the world by her brother, and Eleanor did not begrudge her that. But the fact remained…

Bea was a real lady. Eleanor was not.

And as far the *ton* was concerned, status, birth, mattered.

She might be ward to the Duke, but she was not equal to anyone in this family. Hugh's sense of society and propriety made that clear. She was treated with courtesy, with care. But when she stood with members of the family she felt the gulf between them.

Eleanor was eternally conscious that were it not for the Duke's good graces, the attention she received from men would have a different tenor entirely.

The other was her awareness of that dynamic.

Bea was innocent in a way Eleanor could never afford to be. When her father had died she'd known she was in an extremely precarious place in the world. And it had been his mistress who had explained things to her.

How she had come to be a mistress.

And what it meant when a woman was left in the world without a protector.

She had always liked Missy, but she had known that her relationship with Eleanor's father had been something secret. Eleanor's mother had died when she was a baby, and Missy had been around from the time Eleanor was eight or so.

She knew they were unmarried, yet Missy was part of the household.

She'd asked Missy about that, when the other woman had taken her hand and said to her gravely that she feared the world wouldn't be kind to her.

'Why did you never marry my father?'

Her smile had been sad. 'I'm already married. And my husband's final cruelty to me was to refuse to release me. I never loved another man before your father. I don't know that I'll love any after. But I can own nothing, and so must find a protector who will afford me some comfort.'

'And is that what I will have to do?'

'You can marry, under the right conditions.'

The right conditions had been there in her father's will.

Eleanor was never innocent of what it meant that men coveted her beauty. And when it had been revealed that the Duke of Kendal was to be her guardian it changed everything. For after that, guarding her purity became essential.

She was being given a chance at a far more respectable life than she would have had if left penniless to her own devices.

But she never lost her awareness of it. Or indeed the awareness that many men in the room knew that she was aiming above her station, and that one whiff of scandal would see her falling down to her place. And they would be there to pick her up, and take her to their beds, where they could possess her for nothing more than the promise of their protection and a few trinkets.

The idea made her shiver with distaste.

It was also what made her other impediment to closeness with Beatrice yet more impossible.

She was in love with the Duke of Kendal.

And she might as well have dreamed of sprouting wings and flying to the stars.

She looked in the mirror, at the silver stars woven into her elaborate hairstyle. Her pale pink gown swooping low and hugging the curves of her bosom.

Her beauty didn't matter when it came to Hugh. Which meant it didn't matter much at all. Except that it was a tool. One she could use to get away from him once and for all, which both...distressed and thrilled her all at once.

'The Duke is waiting,' said Hettie.

Eleanor smiled at herself one last time before picking up her reticule and allowing Hettie to drape her pelisse over her shoulders.

By the time she exited her room and made her way down the grand staircase, she was perfectly composed.

Only to see it unravelled by the sight of the Duke of Kendal in front of the entry.

He should be a common sight by now. But there was nothing common about him at all. And there never could be. Dressed all in black, down to the black leather riding gloves that he wore, and the highly polished Hessians on his feet, he was tall and broad, and arrestingly handsome. His blue eyes were like ice chips, his blond hair neatly kept, as if it didn't dare rebel against his will.

That was the thing about the Duke. Everything in his presence obeyed.

Except her heart.

If he had any idea of the things he made her feel…

He would command her heart to stop beating altogether.

But if it were that simple, she would have excised her infatuation with him out of her chest a long time ago.

'I see you are ready,' he said, his eyes raking over her dispassionately.

He was always dispassionate when it came to her.

Even that statement was so carefully neutral. Neither complimentary nor critical. He spoke of her as if she were one of the horses, harnessed and prepared for the journey.

And she realised that she should not be upset about that. She should be grateful that her father had entrusted her care to a man who did not have lecherous intent where she was concerned.

Many men would have taken advantage of a woman in her position. Not because the woman was so beautiful they couldn't control themselves, simply because if they took advantage of an unprotected woman they would face no repercussion.

The only person alive who would defend her honour was Hugh.

He held her fate entirely in his hands, and he had behaved with nothing short of unimpeachable honour. He was a man above reproach. He was a man who would not tolerate even a hint of scandal.

He would never lay a hand on the daughter of a man he had respected, a daughter whose life had been placed into his hands. And he was honourable for it. And she loved him all the same. And wanted nothing more than to have his hands on her body whether he could ever make a marriage between the two of them or not.

And she knew that he could not.

He was a duke. In many ways, nothing was forbidden to him. But it was that very thing that made him all the more courteous. All the more conscientious.

For he was not his father, and never would be.

She knew that much from her friendship with Beatrice.

'As are you,' she said, smiling softly.

Because that was the mask she had to wear. That of a biddable ward.

He couldn't know her. It would leave her impossibly vulnerable. It was a pain she could not fathom. He couldn't know her most shameful thoughts, the deepest part of her.

She had to obey. She had to smile. She had to remain without scandal. She had to make a good marriage so that she could have a life.

Because he would marry eventually.

Because he would need an heir…

She chose not to think about it. But once he had a wife, that wife would not want a grown female ward about the place. Least of all one that was in love with him.

'Let us go,' he said.

And he offered her his arm, because he was a gentleman always. In all things.

And she hated it.

But she took his arm, even though it was tantamount to scalding herself on an open flame, and walked with him out through the door to the waiting carriage.

These rides to the other country homes were always a study in torture. Enclosed in this space with him, barely able to breathe.

Not without smelling the scent of him, sandalwood and his skin, and far too intimate a thing to know about a man she was not married to. A man who was not her family.

And yet, his behaviour towards her was that of an older brother.

That of a guardian.

He would think nothing of it at all. Any more than he thought of Beatrice.

They were ushered into the carriage, the door closed, and her stomach went tight.

'Tonight should be…'

'It will be the same as all the other nights,' she said, unspeakable sadness filling her.

She would be paraded before men she didn't want,

while continuing to reside with the only one she desired.

And then she realised she had spoken out of turn. Her façade had failed her, when she was feeling vulnerable.

She looked at him, gauging his reaction.

His face was flat. 'Indeed.'

'Beatrice would've been excited.'

'Beatrice is off to London with her husband,' he said.

Eleanor knew a moment of envy, and not because Beatrice was off to London at the start of the Season. This was to be her debut. And she had been softly debuting in the country prior to the beginning of the proper Season in London.

She was envious that Beatrice had found love.

Because whatever the circumstances surrounding Beatrice and Briggs's union, she did believe that there was something between them.

She wondered if Hugh thought so. He would never share such a thing with her, obviously.

But no matter what, Beatrice was free now. Of this place. Of this man. Eleanor never would be.

She looked down at his hand, as he tightened it into a fist. The black leather stretching over his knuckles. She swallowed hard. Trying to conceal her breathlessness.

'Still, she might have added a bit more enthusiasm to the trip,' she said. 'I think you and I might be a bit bored of this.'

She didn't know why she was speaking up like

this, but perhaps it was the removal of Beatrice. Perhaps it was the changes. Perhaps it was…

'You and I still have a point and a purpose to these events.'

She was tired, and she had already let her guard down. 'Is that my marriage or yours?'

'Both,' he said.

She stared out of the carriage window, and could see nothing in the darkness. 'You should wait until London.'

'You should not make any declarations until London either. You could do quite well for yourself.'

She turned his words over inside of her. She wondered why he thought so. Because she was beautiful or because she had his money? Perhaps it didn't matter. Perhaps it was both. Equally.

'Wonderful.' And she knew she sounded ungrateful. And that she should endeavour not to. She was quite grateful in many ways.

It was just… It was dark in the carriage, but when their eyes met she felt it. She felt an echo inside her.

She looked away again. 'I imagine you shall find for yourself a diamond of the first water. Whatever leading triumph the Season has to offer.'

'That will depend upon her reputation.'

'You cannot be a diamond of the first water with a tarnished reputation, I would think.'

'You would think.'

Silence settled over them. It was only the horses' hooves on dirt and the carriage wheels turning.

'What will I be?' she asked.

She couldn't help herself. She had to ask the question, because London was drawing near, and she was ever conscious that the men around her felt like wolves. And she had the sensation, ever and always, that if they did not have to marry her, they wouldn't. That if they could have her without making vows to her, low born as she was, they would select that option every time.

'You will do well for yourself.'

Another neutral, carefully selected answer.

'A boon for me, then,' she said.

'It is,' he said, his tone uncompromising. 'What would you do without it?'

'You would throw me onto the streets?' She was teasing. And yet…he could.

She was with him only because he allowed it. Her position was precarious and there was no pretending it wasn't.

Not for her.

Their eyes clashed, and even in the darkness of the carriage she felt something. Sometimes she did, that was the problem. Sometimes when he looked at her, no matter how formal he sounded, no matter how flat his expression, she felt something all the same.

'I am to be engaged before this Season is out. Wed shortly after.'

'And your wife will want me gone.'

'You are my ward,' he said, his tone hard. 'And my responsibility. In that regard it will not matter what she wants. I would never shirk my responsibilities.'

No, of course he wouldn't.

But she was a problem he wanted solved. Whether she could stay under his care for ever wasn't the issue. She did not wish to share a house with Hugh and his wife, she could not.

She'd been given a reprieve when his fiancée had defected last year. And she was grateful for it. She'd been a year away from her Season then, so hadn't had the possibility of beating him to the altar. Now she did.

'Of course you would not.'

The carriage arrived in front of the stately country home of Baron and Baroness Hutchley. She knew the fanfare of arrival now, just as she knew the steps to a dance. Hugh was always courtly with her. Treating her with all the care a guardian should, and yet a certain amount of distance. Just enough that tongues never wagged.

Of course, one look from Hugh and any wagging tongues were sure to be turned to ice, so uncompromising was his gaze, and indeed the man himself.

His hold on her arm was perfunctory as they entered the house and were announced, and yet it still heated her blood. Heated her all the way down.

Her dance card was full nearly the moment she entered the ballroom. And that did not satisfy her, though it should. This was what she should want.

Midway through her second dance she saw Hugh. And the woman he was speaking to.

She was not a woman in her first Season. She was one who had been out for some time, if her memory was correct, and it always was. A woman in Eleanor's position had to know who everyone around her was, with precision.

Anna Paxton.

She was a widow, but one of sterling reputation. And why should a duke be speaking to a widow? She knew there were reasons, but Anna had no whispers of rumour around her when it came to extramarital behaviours.

Hugh had spoken to her at many such occasions. Courting her, she supposed.

Her dance partner must have sensed her distraction. He saw where she was looking. 'Your guardian seems quite taken with Lady Paxton,' he commented.

'Yes,' she said, sure to infuse her tone with deep knowledge.

'I suppose he will be proposing marriage soon. Hopefully it isn't as disastrous as the last one.'

Perversely, that comment upset her. Because Hugh hated to be the subject of gossip, and he had done nothing untoward in his relationship with Penny.

'As long as there are no more marauding Scotsmen around waiting to steal her away, I suppose everything will be just fine.'

It came out more biting than intended, but everything out of her mouth tonight had.

And it was clear by the end of the evening, Hugh had set his intentions on the widow. For he did nothing by accident, and offering his undivided attention to a woman was nothing at all like an accident.

She gritted her teeth through every dance and as

the night ended, she felt gutted. Hollow and hurting and there was no purpose to it. No reason at all.

They got into the carriage together, a perverse pantomime of an attachment they did not have.

'I thought you would wait until London,' she said.

'You said I should. I engaged you in the conversation but I did not say I would.'

'Are you so taken with her?'

'She is reasonable. I am tired of silly young virgins.'

He spoke of his former fiancée, Penny, she was certain. The woman who had run off with the Highlander and broken their engagement, causing a scandal. He spoke of his sister, Beatrice, whose scheme to engineer her own ruin had ended with her marriage to Hugh's best friend.

But she felt it as if it were her he spoke of.

That comment was biting, and it hit her raw and deep. She laughed. She could not help herself. It was that or cry. 'Have you ever thought, Hugh, that they are tired of you?'

She'd used his name. As if she had permission. As if they were intimate.

She waited. For his disapproval. For his censure. To be thrown into the street, as she'd joked before because she could be.

But perhaps there was something in his unravelling that made her braver than she should be. It would all end this Season. He would find a wife, she a husband.

This was it.

It was the end.

'What luck for them, then, that I am soon to be married.'

'What luck indeed,' she whispered. 'What luck indeed.'

'I am sending a note to Lady Paxton, along with flowers. Asking that she come for tea tomorrow. I will expect you to entertain her.'

'Oh, am I to entertain your visitors? How is it I am so lucky? A duchess without the title or the husband. Seeing to the needs of your future duchess.' Again, her heartbreak waged a battle against her control.

And won.

'You are not…'

'What I am not, is a lady of your household. I am not your mother or your sister, and it is not up to me to see to your callers.'

'With Beatrice gone…'

The carriage arrived back at Bybee House. Hugh's mother would be in bed already so they could carry on the conversation without an audience. She did not know if that was a good thing or a bad thing.

She knew this dance too. They would be helped from the carriage, ushered inside, and upstairs to their separate quarters to be readied for bed. Again, so like a couple who were married. Or family. She knew that.

But they were not family and that was a fact that could not be ignored.

They did not follow the steps to the dance, not this time. Once they were in the vast hall, in the middle of the room beneath a beautiful chandelier, and right at the centre of the glorious marble compass just before the stairs, they stood and faced one another.

The members of the household had melted away. Whether signalled by Hugh or sensing they should, she did not know.

But they were alone.

'You will help entertain Lady Paxton tomorrow,' he said throwing his black coat off and draping it over the banister.

There was something about that act, that of him... disrobing in front of her, even if it was his coat, that made her heart catch at the base of her throat.

'And if I don't?'

'Why are you acting the part of naughty child, Eleanor? It doesn't suit you.'

It would be tempting to say their relationship was that of an older brother and a younger sister, but it could never be called that. He occupied a specific position. He was her guardian. The word always conjured up a literal guard in her mind. A man standing sentry, unsmiling and strong, and distant from his charge.

Yet they were required to interact often enough that it could never be quite that simple. For there were times—like this—when they were forced into proximity and that was when it became more difficult.

For her to wear her mask.

For him to remain distant.

That was when it was far too easy for them to spark off each other.

And yet it would be easy for others to compare them to a brother and sister.

But it was not that.

Never that.

'Because I am… I am… I am tired,' she said, finally.

She was. Tired down to her bones. Of wanting this man. Of loving him.

She had loved him now since she was a girl of four and ten. And it was a hideous exhaustion that suddenly draped itself on her like a cloak.

She had always known she couldn't have him, but now, with theirs lives spinning closer to that inevitability it felt so unfair.

Perhaps it was elevated by Beatrice leaving.

There had been so many barriers between them, these many years. Often his friend, the Duke of Brigham was here visiting. Then there was Bea, and for a while there had been Penny, his fiancée.

Tonight it was the two of them, and her own confidante in the house was gone for good from this place and she just…

She was looking at him, and he was looking at her. And it was as if a palpable force stretched between them, as if all that she felt had been made manifest there between them.

The candles in the chandelier blazed, the light catching in the crystals and flickering over his high cheekbones, burning in that sharp blue gaze that should be cold, but warmed her all the same.

She took a step towards him and the heat in his eyes seemed to burn brighter.

'Hugh…'

He hadn't corrected her when she'd used his name. She wondered if he would now.

'Go to bed, Eleanor.'

And then he turned, taking his coat off the banister, and going upstairs. Leaving her to wonder if she had imagined that which had transpired between them.

Leaving her to wonder if the heat was only in her…

Or if he felt it too.

'It wouldn't matter,' she whispered to the bedroom ceiling as she lay there later, unable to sleep.

And that was the saddest truth of all.

Chapter Two

His mother was so socially adept there was never an awkward silence. Anna was deeply pleasant.

Eleanor was the perfect picture of a ward, as he would want one to be. A model of propriety.

And yet.

He would love to say he was bored by the time in the drawing room. But he was never bored when Eleanor was close.

And it was not Eleanor he should be thinking of. But then, it never was. And yet, he always was.

Last night had been an aberration. In that he had possibly allowed her to see some of the effect she had on him. He had not scolded her for using his proper name, and he was furious about it. That she'd said it, and that he'd enjoyed it. The way his name sounded on her tongue.

Last night she had been dressed to attract the attention of a potential husband, the gauzy pink dress she'd worn revealing a tantalising amount of flesh.

Today, her blue dress was nearly prim, her fichu coming up to the base of her throat, and yet it was the knowledge of how that skin looked that fuelled his mind now.

He should be looking at Anna, the woman he had decided to marry. But passion and marriage had never been necessary partners in his mind.

His previous fiancée had been perfect, in that she had been a sweet and kind girl with a spotless reputation. Until she had run off with a Scotsman.

He had been angry about that. But not half so angry as he'd been about the fact his engagement had done nothing to douse the heat he felt for his ward.

Still, he had been set on the marriage.

And since her defection he had been working to get rid of the waves of scandal caused by the broken engagement. And here he was on the verge of another engagement and Eleanor was still all he could think of.

He had chosen Anna because what he'd said to Eleanor was true. He was tired of young women. His sister had nearly caused a massive scandal, and had been railroaded into a marriage of convenience with his best friend. It had to stay one of convenience. Briggs's appetites were not for gently bred women. Least of all his sister, who had medical problems that precluded her from safely giving birth. But Briggs had promised, and given his friend's past, Hugh believed that he would keep his promise.

And though it had all worked out in the end, that

did not mean he didn't find the entire endeavour troublesome.

And going back further, Penny.

As if you were not speaking directly to Eleanor of Eleanor.

She could not possibly know.

She was innocent. She had been under his protection since she was very young, and he had kept her cosseted in his manor house. She was under his care. Lusting after her was a sin, and if hellfire alone had been his primary concern, he might have risked it. But it wasn't simply about hellfire.

His father had been a libertine. And not in the sense that Briggs was. Not even in the sense that Hugh was. He was a man of fierce appetites. It was an issue in some ways, when attempting to be above reproach. But he was circumspect in his affairs.

He made utterly certain that any woman who came to his bed knew exactly what their liaison was.

A business arrangement.

He liked actresses. Women who needed protectors. They understood the situation, and were free with their affections. They had no qualms about the things that he enjoyed. They did not need instruction.

He was not a gentle lover. It was the one place that he had ever allowed himself off the leash. Because once a woman was in his bed the rules had already been laid out clearly. And so it gave him free rein.

Unlike his father, he made the parameters of his desires abundantly clear. He might enjoy a woman in the bedroom, but he would make it plain to her that what they did there would never extend beyond the boundaries of the bed.

But Eleanor could not possibly know that.

The same as she could not possibly know that once she had blossomed into womanhood, his feelings for her had shifted. What had begun as him protecting her from the world had turned into a long rocky road of him protecting her from himself.

The fact was, he was her guardian. Taking advantage of that would not only be shameful, it would be a societal scandal.

And she was the daughter of a merchant. He would marry a woman with a title. A woman who understood the responsibilities of being a duchess. A woman who would make no waves in society.

Touching Eleanor would have set off a wave of utter destruction.

Thankfully, he had ample practice of protecting the world from his baser natures. Things that were bred into him courtesy of his father, he was certain.

He might not know the particulars of what his father had got up to in his bedroom, but around the age of fifteen his own sexual desires had begun to grow into a hunger that had been hard to control. And that, he assumed, was what drove his father.

He had vowed to control the beast.

It was a visit to a French brothel with his best friend Briggs, at sixteen, that had shown him not only what his particular fantasies meant, but how he could express them with responsibility and—yes— even honour.

Many women enjoyed the other side of his particular sexual coin.

And so it was not an imposition to those women, but a gift. In the correct venue, with a partner who shared his desires, he felt no guilt.

Fire was only dangerous outside the hearth. Within, it simply kept you warm.

His father had hurt his mother as if it were a hobby of his. The connection between the two of them had been something beyond his understanding. Intense at times, and then icy. His mother had wept over his father's affairs, but she had not cut him off from her bedroom.

Unlike his father, he kept communication clear with his lovers, and he would never betray his wife. His desires had boundaries. It was how one avoided hurting those they cared for.

His mother was happier now, with his father gone, he was certain of that. But some of the life in her had gone away with him.

Hugh had always found it… Disturbing. Had always found it something he did not want to emulate.

But most of all, his father had made an utter mockery of the title. And everyone he had ever encountered when he'd been a young man had expected him to be the same. It had driven him in the opposite direction. He would not allow his father to dictate what he was. He had endeavoured to carve out a reputation, a new association with the title, and he had succeeded in doing so.

And just as Penny and her defection would not rock his work, neither would Eleanor.

He had meant what he'd said about young virgins.

And there was Anna, who made sense. Because she understood. Because she was different.

She had been married to a titled man before. She had run a household. Her reputation was spotless and he would ensure it remained so. He would court her. He would wed her. He would do so without ever taking liberties, and he certainly wouldn't take lovers while he did so.

He had accepted that his nights spent in brothels with women who shared his sexual tastes were over. All seasons ended. And so this one had ended for him.

He would not keep mistresses once he married. That was a hard line for him.

He had many lines. All drawn around behaviour that mirrored his father's.

'Are you looking forward to your first Season, Eleanor?' Anna posed the question with a smile on her face.

'Oh, yes,' Eleanor said, and just for a moment, her gaze flickered to his. Just a moment, but he didn't miss it. Because he could feel it. 'I am certain that His Grace already has a match in mind for me. And I'm hoping it will be made quickly.'

He knew that she was not really being so biddable, rather, he assumed, she was attempting to needle him. But that would imply that this needled him at all. Last night had been a mistake.

'I feel that His Grace does nothing without a great deal of planning,' Anna responded, in clear agreement.

And he did not like this. These two women conversing about him as if he was not there.

'I would not dream of selecting a suitor for you,' he said. 'The choice should be yours.'

'Choice?' Eleanor asked. 'Are you certain you wish to give me so much freedom? It is entirely possible I could present you with a pirate.'

'And yet, somehow I don't think you will.'

'So certain.'

'About everything.'

'Of course.'

Tension crackled between the two of them. And it was best Eleanor did not know. He chose that moment to take his leave.

'Thank you for calling,' he said to Anna. 'You're welcome to stay and have more tea. I find that I have urgent matters of the estate to attend to. But I hope that you will save me a dance on your card at the Huntingtons'.'

'You know I will, Your Grace.'

But it was not her gaze he felt lingering on him as he left, and as he went to his study to see to his correspondence, it was not her face that he saw in his mind.

It was dinner time before he went downstairs again, and Anna was gone. There was no one in the dining room. He was just about to ask to take dinner in his study, when Eleanor entered the room.

'I didn't expect to find you here,' she said, and backed away as if she intended to leave.

As if she was a lost girl in the forest running away from a wolf.

'You didn't expect to find me in the place where I eat my dinner, at the time when dinner is being served?'

He had done this last night. Pushed her. He should not do it. It was what led to those moments of tension he could not respond to. And yet.

Nothing in his life had ever tested him. He had decided as a boy to be different from his father. And he had been. Always.

When the Duke of Brigham had arrived at school, he'd been bullied horribly for being different. And Hugh had taken Briggs under his wing, at first to prove he was not his father. Because his father had been a vile brute, who would not have showed Briggs any kindness, but rather would have taken joy in making his life a hell.

But soon Hugh had discovered he actually liked Briggs very much, and that his differences made him smart, witty and a hell of a lot more fun than the other aristocratic fools at the school.

It was when he'd made it clear to himself how he would be with women. He had decided, even then, that his actions as the Duke of Kendal would be important. They would set the tone for his heirs, for future generations. His father had given him very little to work with.

And as important as who he was as a duke would be, he had known that his duchess would be equally important. To that end, he'd made a mental list of duchess requirements—and perhaps at fifteen or so the list had been a literal list, which was Briggs's idea, but he was a man with a rather peculiar fondness for order and Hugh had felt he was indulging him—and Hugh was the sort of man who, when making decisions, did so firmly and without wavering.

He had gone with Briggs to a Parisian brothel when they were sixteen and Hugh had purposed to indulge himself in every available vice. Not even so much for the sake of indulgence, but for knowledge.

For experience.

The kind of experience that would inform his actions later. That would inform his interactions with mistresses. That allowed for planning.

He had known even then that when he married he would not seek pleasure outside of the institution, so he had also seen it as the beginning of…burning out his baser instincts.

The type of lady he would marry would not be the sort to engage in his version of pleasure, he knew.

Planning had been the basis for ensuring he was never tempted, knowledge the foundation upon which he built his rather self-righteous set of standards.

He had never been tested until Eleanor. Until the day she had baked him a cake for his birthday. It was a wholly stupid thing. And yet it had been a singular moment in his life.

And it hadn't helped that when she had handed him the cake, she had been wearing a gown that scooped low around her plump breasts and let him see that she was no longer the girl who had first come to live with him, pale and clearly frightened of her own shadow.

She was beautiful. And he had been overcome by the urge to thank her by pressing his mouth to hers. To that sweet, pink mouth that was smiling so brilliantly at him.

Hugh took care of everyone.

It was no less than his duty, and it had been one his father shirked.

His mother was grateful for him. Beatrice loved him. Briggs was loyal to him.

Eleanor had made him a cake.

'Did you really make this?'

'Yes, the cook was cross with me and wished me to leave the kitchen, but I had a mission.'

'Why?'

'If it wasn't for you... I don't know where I would be. Your Grace.'

She had been careful to add *Your Grace*, back then. And last night she had called him *Hugh*.

The urge to touch her had been so strong it had nearly knocked him to his knees. Because he had not ever experienced the deep, driving need to do something he knew he should not.

Everything had a place. A box he could put it in neatly.

Eleanor was a responsibility.

One he took very seriously.

What he did for and to Eleanor would reflect upon him, upon his family. She was an integral piece of his restoration of the title, of his family name.

She was his ward.

And he wanted her.

It had begun that day, this sickness. And it had only got worse.

He vacillated between loathing it, and feeling triumphant in his restraint. After all, had his father wanted to bed the innocent in his care he would have done so. Whether it was wrong or not.

'You went to your study,' she said, coming fully back into the room, a strange, stubborn set to her chin.

'Yes, I did. And now I've come to eat. Sit, Eleanor.'

She did so, but slowly.

'What is it?' he pressed.

'It's strange. Without Beatrice here.'

He had a feeling that was not what made it strange, but he would not be the one to put voice to that.

'She is not here. So strange it will be.'

'I hope she's happy,' Eleanor said, looking down. 'I hope…'

'Theirs will not be a conventional marriage.'

Her head snapped up. 'It won't?'

'You know Beatrice cannot have children. Should not have children, for her health. Briggs has sworn to me he will protect her.'

'And you are…dictating how her marriage will be conducted?'

'It is my duty, Eleanor, to protect those in my care.'

'She's in his care now.'

'Do you think I should take your judgement and feelings into account when I make decisions?' he asked, everything in him hardening.

'You never take anyone's into account, why should you take mine?'

'I am the Duke of Kendal, and all of this is mine. More importantly, it is mine to protect. As is Bea. As are you. A shepherd does not ask his sheep for opinions on their safety.'

She laughed. Eleanor pitched forward at the table. 'I am a sheep to you, is that it?'

'I spoke in metaphor,' he said.

'You did not. You imagine all of us your pure white sheep with you as benevolent shepherd. I do hope you tell Lady Paxton that she is to join your flock. The arrogance.'

'It is not arrogance. It is certainty. Shall I tell you what arrogance looks like? It looks like my father, who did whatever he wished regardless of how it affected those around him. He saw his position as license to treat others however he chose. I care for those around me.'

'It is no different,' she said. 'You do as you see fit. It is only that you see things differently to your father.'

Her words landed like an arrow, right at the centre of his chest. And he had the strongest urge to cross the table and silence her. With his mouth on hers. To teach her a lesson about what manner of man he was beneath everything.

To teach her a lesson of all she was spared from.

But he did not.

And she would never know he was more wolf than

shepherd, for it was the part a man played that mattered. Not what he desired in his heart.

'How is it you have borne my guardianship?' he asked. 'If I am such a trial.'

'A sheep does not tell the shepherd that she would like to run for the hills. She merely plots her escape.'

'Your escape from my money and reputation?' Her breath caught then, her eyes widened. And he could tell that he had struck his mark.

Was the removal of Beatrice all it took to let this rise to the surface? It wasn't as if he never sparred with Eleanor. They were isolated here at Bybee House, out in the country, and they had of necessity spent a fair amount of time in each other's company.

Though Hugh often returned to London while the women remained at the estate.

Still, it was not usually like this.

He knew the reason for the tension between them. He could see that she did not.

'Do not worry, my shepherd,' she said softly. 'My manner of escape will be one that meets with your approval. I will find a husband by the end of the Season. And you will be rid of the burden of me once and for all.'

Chapter Three

A final party before London.

Maybe she would find a husband here? Why wait until London at all? Maybe she would run away with a pirate.

She knew she wouldn't.

She was all but boiling in her indignation as she sat in the carriage next to Hugh, her mint-coloured gown creasing at the fold of her lap because she could not stop worrying at it with her nervous fingers.

She was not nervous about the party. She was… next to him and things had not been well since the day Lady Paxton had visited.

She had behaved badly, she supposed. But his high-handedness had been… In character. He was a duke, after all.

True.

But more than that, he was Hugh Ashforth, the Duke of Kendal, and he was a supremely arrogant man down to his very bones. She thought that were he a merchant he would likely possess the same manner of arrogance that he did as a duke.

Impossible to say.

But she felt she did know.

In her heart.

Which was far too concerned with him.

A sheep.

He had called her a sheep…

She wanted to marry a pirate to spite him. But she knew she had the chance to make a marriage a girl of her station would otherwise not be able to make.

It was imperative.

Her parents were dead.

She could not remember her mother. Her father… She had loved him so very much. He would have seen her cared for, she knew it. But his money could not pass to her. It could not pass to the mistress he'd loved. The woman who couldn't marry him because she had been forced into a marriage with a cruel man when she was very young, and never released from that marriage.

The greatest gift Eleanor had been given was this guardianship. In the sense that it opened up a measure of possibility she would not have had without it.

She would be a wife to a man of her choosing, and she would have more men to choose from because of Hugh and that… That would be the legacy of him. Of living with him. Of caring for him…

How ironic that it was he who would be key to her finding a husband.

'You must endeavour to look less angry with me,' he said.

'I'm not angry,' she said.

She was lying. She was angry. And several other things, all tangled together at the centre of her breast like a bright ball of anguish, but she did not have the energy to continue with it all. She would rather lie and have it be all right.

'You are not an accomplished liar.'

She let out a long sigh and she didn't care right now whether or not she was biddable. 'Why would I be?'

In the darkness of the carriage she could feel him looking at her. And the moment stretched. She could hear their breath and it was so deeply, strangely intimate to hear their breathing mingled in that way that for a moment she lost her sense of the ceiling and floor of the carriage. For a moment everything felt…turned.

And so did she.

Bea was no longer here to offer a buffer, but she sensed it was more than that. It was the ending of all this, looming in sight, creating an edge of desperation within her.

'No reason at all.'

They arrived then. Thank God.

And the arrival itself was a blur. All that mattered were the moments they'd been alone, while this was all frightfully, horribly bland.

Dance cards and indistinguishable men in the same uniform of breeches, boots and waistcoats. She supposed she should count herself lucky. She attracted the attention of young men, and the older men seemed to know she was not yet at a place where she had need of an arrangement quite so imbalanced.

And that was Hugh. All Hugh.

The knowledge did not make her less angry.

For his part, Hugh's attention was set only on Lady Paxton. She looked over the shoulder of her current dancing partner and saw him with his head bent low, talking to her. Was he being amusing? He could be, she knew that. But he so rarely was.

As if a smile cost him dearly. As if levity might break him.

As if he had to be on guard at all times.

Defending the duchy and its reputation or…she didn't know. He was a man of so much power, wealth and influence. If she had that, all on her own, she might flout convention a little.

But just the thought of flouting convention made terror take flight in her breast.

The thought was…like falling. And as she was already feeling out of balance from the carriage ride perhaps she should think less of falling while she was trying to dance, with a man who might well be very nice but who was something like porridge when compared to Hugh.

Other women agreed, she could see it in the way they looked at him.

There was an avarice to their gazes, and it was deeper than money.

She remembered her father's mistress telling her in no uncertain terms that what a man wanted from a woman was physical. That she felt it was unfair for Eleanor to be unaware of what transpired between a man and a woman as it was essential to the outcome of a woman's life.

There were few options for women, she'd said. You would either sell yourself one time to your husband, or many times over to your protectors.

'Your body is a commodity. And no man wants his goods to be used. I was lucky with your father, after a deeply unhappy marriage. But I was unlucky in the years between and I have no guarantees after. You must seek security. You can be ruined by being alone with a man. By his kiss, by his touch. Most of all, you must remain a maid. Once a man puts his prick inside of you then you are ruined. There are ways to feign innocence, you can try. But what matters most of all is what people know.'

The blunt lesson in relations between men and women had confused her at the time. In the years since, with access to the library at Bybee House, she had managed to piece together the truths of it.

That was what those women were hungry for. With Hugh.

She had tried, for a very long time, to never think of those things in connection with him. Her heart ached when she looked at him, and he made her shiver.

Made her feel unsteady.

But she was almost afraid the very thought of it would be her ruin and the simple truth was: She would never be the Duchess of Kendal.

He would never marry her. It would be unsuitable in every way, as *she* was unsuitable. His current choice for the position of duchess spoke to that loudly. As did his previous choice. Penny had been the daughter of an earl, and even that was close to being beneath him.

Eleanor was nothing.

She was his ward, that was all.

But still, she could see that no man in this room possessed the magnetism that he did. He was a golden flame, his features sharp and sculpted. Uncommonly tall and broad, he was the perfect figure of masculine grace and strength. While many other men with his wealth and status frittered it away on drinking and rich foods, spent their days indulging themselves and steeping themselves in malaise, Hugh was always active. Always on the move.

He took personal interest in his estate, and he worked with his hands.

He was a rarity and it was clear.

And she had spent another two whole dances without being aware of her partner. She had, in fact, changed partners and not even noticed because both men were slim with light brown hair and navy waistcoats, roughly three inches taller than her own height.

She made eye contact with her current partner. 'It is a glorious night,' she said, altogether too brightly.

He seemed shocked she had spoken. 'Uh…yes.'

'A wonderful party.'

'Quite.'

'Do you like parlour games?'

He seemed utterly taken aback by her suddenly pointed conversation, and truthfully, she was slightly taken aback by it as well. But she was tired of staring at Hugh and tired, in general, of everything being about Hugh and she needed to find a husband. That conviction had grown stronger since last evening. Burned in her like a fire threatening to rage out of control.

And if she was going to marry, she would choose the man.

So she needed a list of priorities. The top being that he could provide for her. She would not marry a pauper. She would not dishonour what her father had given her by choosing a husband who could not care well for her and surely no one could think less of her for that.

If she had won some sort of prize in gaining Hugh as her guardian then she would make sure it was the shiniest of prizes.

After all, it was a pot of winnings getting her the husband she would one day find, wasn't it? The ear of the Duke, some of his money, and an untouched bride.

She was providing the untouched, unspoiled goods.

In her opinion they were worth quite a lot.

If everyone in society insisted on attaching value to a woman's body, why shouldn't she, and make it work for her?

'I'm not certain what you mean.'

'Charades,' she said.

'Is someone playing charades?'

'Not to my knowledge.' She smiled.

'You know,' he said, suddenly looking thoughtful. 'I think I might know of some parlour games being played.'

That had not been her aim per se, but it was interesting enough.

'All right,' she said.

'Shall we slip away?'

He had been attentive and polite so far, and they were talking about going to another area of the party, so she did not see the harm in it. She should…

She should ask Hugh's permission.

Like he was her father.

The idea galled her.

And he was still talking to Lady Paxton.

'Lead the way,' she said, allowing him to whisk her from the dance floor. They wove through the ballroom and through the crowded corridor. There were guests everywhere which made her feel secure.

Even as they wound their way up the curved staircase she still didn't think ought was amiss, but when he ushered her into the study it was…empty.

'You said…'

And then he advanced on her. 'I believe I correctly interpreted your meaning?'

'No. You didn't.'

'I didn't?'

'I like charades, Lord Elston, I do not like being herded into empty darkened rooms.'

'You actually meant charades?'

'I am very good at them.'

'Perhaps you will prove good at this too.'

He moved towards her and she stepped away, and then he lunged for her. She whirled around and grabbed hold of an ink pot on the desk behind her and swung it around, bringing it into direct contact with the side of his head…

Just as Hugh walked into the room.

'What in the devil is going on?' He grabbed Lord Elston and shoved him back against the wall. 'Leave. Now. And if you breathe one word to anyone I will end you. Your every connection, your reputation. Everything. Do not think you will come out of this ahead simply because you are a man and she is a woman. She is a woman under my protection. And that puts her leagues ahead of you.'

He shoved Elston out through the door and then strode towards her. Her heart was thundering and she was still filled with fire and…and bees in her blood, because it was hot and it buzzed. And then he touched her. His hands were on her upper arms and they were…they were shockingly rough on her skin and now she couldn't breathe.

'Did he hurt you?'

'I think I hurt him. He will be going back into that ballroom with a lump on his head.'

'What in the hell were you thinking, Eleanor?'

His blue eyes were a flame and his touch on her skin was too much. His proximity was too much. All of it was too much.

'He told me there were games and I believed him. I…'

'You have to be smarter than that,' he said, lowering his voice to a whisper, rough and insistent. 'I saw you leave with him, what if someone else did?'

'There were people,' she protested, but it was feeble. 'All the way until he led me in here there were people. We were alone for a moment...'

'A moment is all it takes.'

'I thought it took several moments for a man to debauch a woman.'

He drew back. 'You don't know anything about how precarious a position you're in, then.'

And that was too much. Her temper exploded. 'I don't know anything about the position I'm in? You're wrong, Hugh. I am well aware. I am here only because of you. I have a means to a good marriage only because of you. Because of your money. I am only protected from what just happened because of you. If not for you I might be a governess, if I were lucky. If I weren't so lucky the mistress of a much older man by now. I do know how the world works. I am not from your station, do not forget that. My father might have been a wealthy enough merchant, but all of that money went to male relatives and none for me, and there is not even a title to offer me protection. It's only because you knew him. Only because you took an interest in my fate. But please know I am well aware what else lies out there in the world for me.'

'Then you must endeavour to be more careful.' He drew away, straightening the lapels on his jacket and extending his arm as if he was going to escort her in as he'd done in the beginning.

'Perhaps men such as Lord Elston should endeavour to be more human and less like vile serpents.'

He lowered his arm. 'I agree with you, but the simple truth is, they won't. Do you think women choose ruin, Eleanor? Society chooses it for them, and they could have chosen it for you tonight if the wrong person had seen this.'

Her heart was pounding and she suddenly felt dizzy. Sick.

He was right and she knew it. He extended his arm again, and this time, she took it.

'The sooner we get to London the better. We need to get you married off.'

And she tried to smile as he whisked her down the stairs and back into the ballroom, as if nothing had happened. But her heart was still pounding, and her arm still burned where he had touched her.

Chapter Four

They were off to London today and Hugh was in a vile temper. Last night he… He would have committed a murder if he'd not been thinking clearly of Eleanor's reputation. When he'd walked into the room and seen Elston's hands on her…

And then he'd seen her neatly defend herself.

He was impressed by that, but much less impressed that she'd been gullible enough to allow that man to lure her from the ballroom.

She had not been forthcoming about what had led to that string of events, but he intended to speak to her about it at some point.

Their trunks were being loaded up into one carriage and they would ride in another.

His mother's lady's maid was sitting with her in the parlour and he turned to her. 'Abigail, I do not see my mother's trunk.'

'Oh… Your Grace…'

'It is not packed,' his mother said.

'It needs to be packed. We must depart in the next twenty minutes. We cannot be caught on the road after dark, the coaching inn is five hours from here.'

'I am aware of the route you favour to get to London,' his mother said.

When he went to London alone he rode his horse and took it in a day, most often. But with carriages laden with trunks there was no way to make it without stopping.

'Then why are you not prepared,' he said, trying to smile.

He did not like it when things didn't go according to schedule.

'I have decided I am not going.'

'Mother, Beatrice is in London.'

'It has been a mere week since I've seen her, Hugh, and while I do miss my only daughter, I've decided the London Season is no longer appealing. I prefer to rusticate.'

'If you wish to sit, sit in my town house.'

'I will not subject myself to the journey to a city I've no wish to spend time in.'

He stared at his mother. She had only grown more and more stubborn with each passing year. He had no idea what had caused it. 'Mother, what about Eleanor?'

'She is your ward, Hugh, not mine. And she is a lovely girl. You will have no trouble finding her a match whether or not I'm there.'

'Do you not think it stretches propriety for her to make this journey with me?'

'And a variety of household staff. You are a man above reproach. If it was your father? Perhaps no one would trust that he was caring for a ward. But no one would ever think that you would take advantage of anyone in your care.'

That made something land, hard, in the centre of his chest. 'Thank you,' he said.

He wasn't altogether certain that was the appropriate response. And it was not often he was uncertain.

'Give Beatrice my love. I do hope she's faring well with her new husband…'

'Briggs will treat her right.' Of that he was certain.

'I'm glad to hear you express such confidence in him.'

'You've known Briggs since he was a schoolboy.'

'And I do not trust easily, life has seen to that.'

'But you trust me,' he said.

'I do. And you must know, that is not given lightly.'

He looked at his mother, and noticed the lines around her eyes. The grey at her temple. She had aged, and yet she didn't seem weak. She appeared stronger than ever.

'And I thank you for that. But I do wish you would come to London.'

He would have no buffer between Eleanor and himself and he could still feel her soft, creamy skin beneath his fingers if he thought too hard about it. Or really, even if he thought about it not at all.

It was still there.

It burned.

'It is a good thing to be missed,' she said. 'Especially at my age.'

He leaned down and kissed her cheek, before straightening and heading back out into the hall, where Eleanor was standing, watching the servants bustle with trunks.

'My mother has decided to stay home for the Season. We will go to London without her.'

'Oh,' Eleanor said, her eyes round.

'No need to look frightened.'

Though she did and he wondered if she was anticipating him taking her to task once they were alone in the carriage.

Which was fair. Since he was absolutely going to.

He noticed she made herself scarce after that. A little blue silk ghost, floating around the periphery of the action.

Avoiding him.

Until she couldn't any longer.

'We always find ourselves in carriages,' she said, once they were closed inside.

'We are always going somewhere.'

'Where will we stop tonight?'

'A coaching inn about five hours down the road.'

He could see her visibly shrink when he said that. As if five hours with him might kill her.

'Get it over with,' she said.

'What?'

'Your lecture.' The carriage lurched forward, then began to sway gently back and forth as they started down the road.

'I did not say I had a lecture for you.'

'But you do! I can see it glimmering behind your eyes. So why don't you tell me how foolish I am, and how men cannot be trusted and how I must be more mindful of my reputation.'

'Why should I do that? You've just said it all.'

'You want to.'

'Contrary to what you may think, Eleanor, I do not actually live to lecture you.'

'Do you not?'

'I have other things to do. It is simply that you and Beatrice have often required a fair amount of lecturing.'

Eleanor rested her chin on her hand and gazed out of the window, her delicate profile so lovely in the early afternoon light it nearly stole his breath. He was used to heat. He was not used to this. This gentle desire that filled him, which seemed to be about more than lust.

'You worry about her,' she said, turning to look at him.

And it was like she had brought in all the sun from outside that window and pushed it straight into his chest.

'Worry is not active,' he said.

'But you do.'

'She was very sick. For a long time.'

'I remember some of that,' Eleanor said.

Bea had been mostly abed in those years. Physical activity or even the wrong trees or plants seemed to leave her gasping for air. Illness struck her harder than it did others. A sniffle for Bea seemed to inevitably go to her compromised lungs and cause her to spend days fighting for breath. Fighting for life.

Hugh was a man who prized control above all else. And when he looked at Bea, he saw all in this world he could not control.

'If he does anything that might harm her...'

'You think he might?'

'Men are weak, Eleanor.'

'Not you, though,' she said, softly.

'No. I have never been allowed to be. My father had enough weakness for three men. Someone had to compensate.'

'But you think Briggs weak?'

'I think him human.'

'In a way you don't see yourself?'

Why did she have to needle him? She was pushing the bounds of his strength and she had no idea. 'That is not what I mean. But he has taken her as his wife.' He should not speak of such things with her. She had been naïve enough to be led from the ballroom...

And she was canny enough to have shifted the conversation well away from that. She had told him exactly what he would say and had made him sound boorish even to himself and then she had managed to turn the topic to him.

'Why exactly did you follow him from the ballroom?'

'What does that have to do with Bea and Briggs?'

'Nothing. And yet we are talking about them and I think that is by your design.'

Her eyes widened. 'No! I was merely taking note of the distress you feel about your sister because I do know you and...'

'Why did you leave with him?'

'I'm embarrassed to say.'

Dear God, if she was going to talk to him about desire and quickening pulses he was going to jump out of the carriage.

'Say it anyway.'

'I thought we were going to find a game of charades.'

And that was so unexpected that he, the Duke of Kendal, who never laughed if he could help it, pitched forward and let out a bark of laughter so loud he wouldn't be surprised if it frightened whole flocks of birds as they passed.

'Do not laugh at me!' she asked. 'I said I liked parlour games, charades in particular, and he...'

'Took you up on what he thought was an innuendo.'

'It wasn't!' she insisted.

'I know. But he didn't.'

She looked furious then. 'Are you defending him?'

'Absolutely not. When I walked in it was clear you were a woman in distress, and whatever he thought leading up to that moment he had ample evidence that you did not wish to be touched by him, and he should have led you back to the ballroom, as a gentleman. But sadly, gentlemen are not common enough. Merely snakes who wear waistcoats, and they are everywhere.'

She seemed to ponder that for a moment. 'And you do not trust anyone.'

'I have seen too much of what men are willing to do to satisfy themselves. And there are few limits to it. My entire life is an attempt to correct the wrongs of the man who came before me. The sins of the father are visited on the son. Unless the son does all he can to be above reproach.'

'My father was a good man.'

'He was.'

'How did you meet him?'

They had never spoken of this. Perhaps because they rarely spoke of anything serious. Anything of depth, and why would they? She was his ward. She was friends with his sister, a good companion to his mother. Without Bea around they had spoken with much more frequency because his vibrant sister wasn't there to be a barrier.

In all this time, they'd never spoken of her father.

'When I inherited the duchy my father had left much in disarray. Perhaps the most scandalous thing I have ever done is endeavour to earn some of the wealth back that he had squandered. I invested heavily in many of your father's merchant ventures and it was successful. Then he died and you inherited none of it, all the wealth going to male relatives. Me? I had profited greatly off all he had done and... I considered him a friend, though I was many years his junior. He made me believe that there were honest men in the world. He loved you a great deal. And when his illness took hold and he asked that I see to your care it seemed such a small thing to ask after all he had done.'

He had never spoken of this to anyone, not even his mother. Not even Briggs. He had never admitted to the extent of the ruin the estate and the finances had been left in. He had built it all back up and then some. It was more than simply a reputation he had to salvage. It was their very survival.

He could have married a wealthy woman. He did know that. But his pride prevented it. It felt too much like something his father would have done— had done, in fact.

Marry a woman for a dowry.

Marriage might be an exchange of favours, but his conscience would not allow him to engage in that exchange.

A woman with a sterling reputation, that was all he wanted.

A woman who could enhance the work he was doing.

Not a woman he needed, not in that way.

'I am not such a joyless burden, then,' she said.

'I never said you were.'

'Your manner suggests it at times.'

'I will tell you it was joyless to find you in that idiot's embrace. How about that?'

She went scarlet and for a moment he wondered if he'd betrayed something. He hadn't meant it in the way it could potentially be misconstrued. He was not a jealous man. He'd never had reason to be. If he wanted a woman, he bought her.

That might sound callous, but it was so.

He could not afford distraction and so turning his affairs into transactions was the best course of action. One woman or another, it did not matter.

He'd only meant she'd created a problem for him.

'If you ruin yourself I will not be able to find you a proper match.'

And then she went beetroot. *'If. I. Ruin. Myself?'* She practically launched herself across the carriage to the seat directly beside him. 'Tell me, Hugh, was a man not there? Did a man not instigate the entire thing? Was he not the one who led the charge in my potential ruination whilst I… I fended him off! And you, with all your umbrage, were late.'

'You nearly lost your virtue over the promise of a pantomime.'

'I would not… I would never… And I…' She was huffing and nearly choking on her outrage. 'I would like to pantomime choking you to death, only slip up and accidentally do it in truth.' She reached out and put her hand on his throat. Her palm was soft. Her fingers were soft.

She was so angry. Like a puffed-up little cat, all feral claws and teeth. But too small to do much harm.

Still, her touch against his skin…

Without gloves.

Damn.

He was not a green boy and she was not a seductress. Not even close.

'Darling,' he said. 'I do not let women do the choking.'

She withdrew her hands quickly, her eyes round. 'I don't know what you mean.'

He shifted, regretting his choice to engage her this way. 'Nor should you.'

He was inordinately relieved when they arrived at the coaching inn. 'Wait here,' he said.

He got out, feeling grateful to no longer be sharing the space with her. He went inside and found it crowded, the noise unbearable. 'Excuse me,' he said to a woman moving quickly past him with two trenchers of ale in hand. 'I require two rooms for the night.'

The woman laughed while looking him up and down. 'You only get one, but I'll let you pay double for it, looking as fine as you do.'

'I have need of two,' he said.

'We only have the one. The finest one, ain't been rented out yet because no one can afford it. Though I'm sure you can.'

'I'll take it,' he said, jaw clenched tight. 'My wife and I…'

He didn't know why in the hell he'd said that. He wasn't going to share a room with her. He'd sooner sleep in the barn. And he damn well would.

He was a man who prized honour and she was to be untouched.

But she laughed. 'Call her whatever you like, luv, I don't care either way. Last door at the end of the corridor.'

Tension crept up his spine as he went back to the carriage. 'Come,' he said, holding his hand out.

Eleanor's eyes widened, but she extended her hand and curled her dainty fingers in his. And he remembered her touch against his throat. He looked at hers. Pale and silken, her pulse thundering hard at the base of it.

He looked away.

He all but dragged her inside and he knew he was not treating her as he should. But this was all a bit much.

He refused to call it too much.

Nothing yet in his life had been too much.

One small woman would never be too much.

They went up the stairs and he continued to pull her—firmly—down the corridor before shoving the door open and revealing a very spare room with a wide bed that was clearly intended to be shared.

'This is yours,' he said.

He turned and examined the large plank of wood that would serve as a bar for the door. The thing that would protect her. God in heaven, this was untenable. Rather than being only down the corridor from her he would have to be outside, and leave her here to whatever rough element was staying in the place.

Or he could sleep in front of the door.

On the floor.

Surely that would be acceptable.

In society, of course it would not be, but no one would have any idea of their sleeping arrangements at the coaching inn, and as for his conscience, it would be clear enough.

'They have but one room,' he said, his words clipped.

Eleanor's mouth went slack. 'Oh.'

'I am happy to sleep in the stables, my concern however is that this room is not secure enough for my liking. And I care much more for your actual protection than I do for the protection of reputation.'

'They are one and the same,' she said, her voice sounding thick. 'Are they not?'

'In some cases. But not in this one. Did you not see how many rowdy drunks are down there? If anyone knew you were up here alone…'

'What are you proposing, that we share this bed?'

That brought to mind images of her silken skin beneath his hands and that was unacceptable.

'No,' he ground out. 'I am suggesting I sleep by the door. In front of it. As a literal barrier between you and anyone who means you harm.'

'But if anyone finds out…'

'I know,' he said, his jaw tight.

'You put too much stock in your reputation, Hugh. How far can it possibly go?'

'You cannot call me that,' he said.

She turned pink again. 'I'm sorry, I…'

'You keep slipping up. In London that will not be acceptable. In London we cannot have familiarity such as that.'

'Perhaps you should sleep in the barn,' she bit out. 'I think I would rather take my chances with the drunkards.'

'You know nothing.'

Their trunks were brought up and he made no comment to his staff, nor would he. Instead he took his nightshirt from the trunk and rolled it up, throwing it down to the roughhewn floor.

'What are you doing?' she asked.

'Sleeping.'

Leaving on his boots, his coat, everything, he lay down on the floor, his back firmly to her, his head on the shirt.

'This is ridiculous,' she said.

'Ready yourself for bed and speak not to me again.'

He heard no movement, not for a long while. Then he heard the trunk, the rustling of fabric. And he gritted his teeth as he tried not to walk through which layer of clothing she might be removing. As he tried not to imagine how she might look.

Then he heard the bedclothes.

It was not a relief.

Knowing she was mere feet from him in her nightgown, in bed.

Eleanor.

His Eleanor.

For some reason that echoed in his mind until he slept.

And when he woke, cold and stiff on the floor, it was his first thought.

What a disastrous journey.

Chapter Five

Eleanor could barely look at him the next morning. She was awash in fury and humiliation.

A duke had slept on the floor, in front of the door to keep her safe.

In any other circumstances she might have found that…

She did anyway. She didn't look at him as the carriage rolled into London, to the town house that he kept for his time spent in the city.

The problem was, she felt…

Confused.

Touched in some way that he had done that to protect her physically, even though she knew it had chafed at his sense of honour.

But she also felt scalded by his rebuke at her use of his given name, even though she had known all along she was pushing the bounds of propriety by speaking it. And then there had been the act of taking her dress off while she could hear him breathing.

Knowing he was there.

She had turned away from him as if it might offer dual protection, but she had looked over her shoulder once, only once, as she had allowed her innermost undergarments to fall from her body.

He had been facing away still, resolute.

She hadn't known what she felt about that. She should feel pleased. He was honourable, and he had proved himself to be.

Instead she felt almost wounded.

She could not help but wonder what it would have been like to have him lie in bed beside her. And the thought had kept her from truly being able to sleep at all. She would squint through the darkness, trying to see if she could make out his form against the door, still lying there.

And it was all tangled up in her hurt and anger at him and mostly she wondered if she was simply sad. That this was coming to an end.

That she would not be in his household any more and as that ended so would the deep, dark fantasies that lived inside her.

Fantasies she had always known were outlandish and had no place in the order of things.

Fantasies she had always known must be kept shoved down inside her.

But living with him as she did it was easy to pretend.

That he was hers.

He was not.

He never would be.

The very first reason was that he was a duke, and he could belong to no one. Least of all a girl of low birth who had nothing at all to her credit except for his good favour.

And it wasn't even good favour she'd earned.

It was down to what he'd felt for her father.

'Are you not elated to be in London?' he asked, his voice dry.

He knew full well she was not.

'Ecstatic,' she responded. 'We draw ever nearer to my finding a husband.'

'We will go and see Beatrice this afternoon, would you like that?'

He sounded nice then. Gentle as if he were speaking to a child, and she preferred to fight him. But she decided to maintain the façade that all was well.

'I would, thank you.' Then she looked at him. 'It has been very lonely without her.'

The town house was a stately home with white-washed brick and wrought-iron balconies, climbing with brilliant pink roses.

The entry was grand with white and black marble laid out in a spiral pattern, and a gilded chandelier with glimmering candles. The curved staircase was wide, with rich mahogany banisters, yet more evidence of the duke's status.

Just more evidence of the gulf between them.

In a coaching inn, as preposterous as it was, the gap between them felt narrowed. Especially with him sleeping on the floor.

Here it could not be more clear.

Especially when he stepped inside behind her and removed his gleaming black top hat from his head, looking like he might have been fashioned out of the same fine materials as his home. Cold marble and priceless gold.

Untouchable.

Beyond reach.

Even with this gulf between them, she felt drawn to him. And that was the most absurd thing. Why should she feel a pull towards a man who occupied the stars?

Yet she did.

Being with him was pain. A study in torture.

And the idea of being without him felt like devastation.

'You will be shown to your room. Change into something fresh and we will be on our way to Bea and Briggs's town house.'

She wanted to ask him if that was strange. His sister now living with his friend.

But he had warned her against familiarity. She felt like he needed someone to reach out to him now, and out of spite she didn't.

He didn't give her what she needed. Why should she give any to him?

Instead, she went to change her dress and get ready to face Bea.

She went with the blue dress, because it made her feel serene. And she desperately needed some serenity after that carriage trip.

But what she wasn't prepared for was the full impact of Hugh, dressed smartly to the standards of London society, which was quite different—she suddenly realised—to the degree he dressed in the country.

He was resplendent. And she hated him for it.

'Are you ready?'

'Do I not look ready, Hugh?'

And she was prepared for it. The biting retort that was about to fly out of his mouth. Because she had baited him. And still, she flinched.

'You would do well to remember where we are.'

'Shall I forget, then, that you slept on the floor in my bedchamber last night?'

'Your Grace,' he said, his voice low and dangerous, and she was disappointed that she could not continue to push. Continue to bait. Because it would've made her feel better. Or maybe it wouldn't have. But it would've made him feel worse. And that... That seemed reasonable.

He extended his arm, and she did not take it. Instead she walked ahead of him out of the door and got into the carriage. He didn't comment on her lack of propriety. He simply got in behind her. Wordlessly.

They were quiet on the short trip down the row of beautiful town houses and over several streets to where Briggs and Beatrice made their home.

They were greeted by a butler who might've been identical to the one in residence at Hugh's home, and while Hugh was ushered towards what was undoubtedly Briggs's masculine study, Eleanor went to Beatrice's morning room. Her friend wasn't there. She

sat, looking around the space, which was delicate
and lovely, and she wondered if Beatrice liked being
in London. If she had found something here that she
hadn't been able to find back in Bybee House. Beatrice had always been so restless. Had always been
desperate for adventure, and there had been none to
be had at Bybee House.

The truly perverse thing was that Eleanor had
never wanted adventure. She'd wanted to be safe.

And she wanted Hugh.

Well. She could have safety. So there was that.

'Eleanor,' Beatrice said as she walked into the
morning room. She crossed the room quickly and
embraced Eleanor, who hugged her friend back, surprised by the rush of emotions that filled her. They
hadn't truly been apart from each other in so many
years, and these last few days had been strange and
trying.

She loved her friend, for her own merit. But the
fact remained that she had been a convenient buffer
against Hugh, and the loss of that was something that
Eleanor had felt greatly.

'How are you?' Beatrice asked. 'Please tell me that
Hugh isn't being an ogre.'

An ogre? She thought of how he been these past
days. The volatility between them. The way that he
had slept on the floor. The way that he scolded her.
The way that he looked at her. The way it felt when
he touched her arm.

'No more so than usual.' She looked away. Because

she was sure that Beatrice would be able to see all of it written on her skin.

'What's wrong?'

'Nothing,' she said, attempting to keep her tone bright. 'I'm here for the Season. I will find a husband. That is a good thing.'

It was. It would stop this. All this confusion. All this madness. This useless longing that led to something she could never have.

'Yes,' Beatrice said. 'If it is what you want.'

Beatrice sounded wholly doubtful, and it wasn't fair. Beatrice might suspect something about her feelings for Hugh, but what she didn't understand was the reality that Eleanor found herself in. Beatrice could play games. She could fling herself at men in drawing rooms to be purposefully ruined, and still come out married to a duke. Eleanor could do no such thing.

'I'm not like you, Beatrice. I do not have an assured place in this world whether I marry or not.' Her breath caught in her throat. 'I'm sorry. That was not a kind thing to say. I know that Hugh demanded you not marry.' But still. Control meted out by her brother was not the same as facing a life where one wrong move would make her a fallen woman.

'I'm not angry.'

Just then the doors to the room opened, and the maid came in with a tea service on a rolling tray. She laid it out before them. Beautiful, lovely sandwiches and cakes, the kinds of things that Eleanor had become accustomed to since joining the Duke's household. Things she was not entitled to. Not in the way that Beatrice was.

Beatrice smiled. Enigmatically. 'I like being married.' And then her cheeks went pink. 'I mean... I like... I'm pleased that I get to host you in my own home.'

But Eleanor could sense subtext beneath it all. The sort that she herself was grappling with. 'And what of Briggs?' She asked. Because she had to wonder what it was like for her to share a home with Hugh's shameless friend. And his child. Beatrice had gone from being a cosseted, spoiled young thing to being a wife and mother. Eleanor couldn't deny that she felt a surge of jealousy.

'He is... I care for him a great deal, Eleanor.'

Yes. Eleanor knew about that kind of care. 'Of course you do,' she said. 'You always have.'

Beatrice took a bite of sandwich, and sat there looking conflicted. She shifted, almost squirming in her seat. And then her next words seemed to burst forth from her. 'I want to speak to a doctor again. About having a baby.'

The words hit her like an anvil in her chest. 'But they said you could not.'

'I know. But I... I have been with him. Intimately.'

And now she was well and truly jealous. Along with being shocked, and afraid for her friend's safety. She could be with child already. 'Beatrice...'

'It could not... We could not... You don't understand, Eleanor. He is the other half of me. I...'

She did understand. It was just that regrettably

Hugh was not the other half of her, and he never could be. He was just a dream. As far out of reach as the stars in the sky. As untouchable as the moon.

He was everything to her. And she was nothing to him.

And maybe Beatrice was naïve. Maybe Briggs was not her other half. Maybe it was simply that Beatrice wished to touch the sky. And always had.

Eleanor had never thought that about herself. But she did. It was true.

'You're in love with him,' Eleanor said softly.

That statement did not seem to make Beatrice happy. 'I had hoped,' she said slowly, 'that love would feel nicer.'

She was *married* to the man she was *in love with*. Did it still hurt so much?

'Is he not nice?'

'He is… I cannot explain him. But please don't tell Hugh about us.'

Well, as much as she might be jealous of the situation with her friend, she didn't think it was Hugh's business. And she had been categorically against his attempt to control her from the beginning. 'You are married,' she said. 'If he honestly thinks he's going to control the way that you and Briggs are with one another now that you are… Now that you are married.'

'Just please do not tell him. He wanted Briggs to act as his stand-in, but it is not… That is not how we are with one another. I am not his ward. I'm his wife. I do not know if I love him. I… He makes me feel as if my heart is being cut out of my chest sometimes. And like I might die if I cannot be near him.'

I am not his ward. I am his wife.

And that was true. It was the truth of it. And Eleanor was Hugh's ward. There was no prettying it up. There was no changing it. There was nothing that could be done.

'I feel like I might die if I cannot be near him...'

'And you won't be. He will marry Anna. You will marry another. Your whole life, you won't be near him. And you are not his sister. Once you are wed will he seek you out at all? Will he ever speak to you again?'

'As I understand it,' she said, the words coming out whether she wanted them to or not, 'that is love.'

Beatrice looked at her, for far too long. 'You are in love with my brother,' she said.

She felt bleak. Hopeless. Beatrice could see it. Maybe Hugh could see it as well. Maybe everybody could. Perhaps she was the laughing stock of all of England. 'It is impossible.'

'It is only impossible because you think it is, and there is nothing that can be done once my brother decides something. That is the only reason, and it is not a very good one.'

Eleanor swallowed, and felt as if her throat was lined with a bag of prickles. 'I should hope that you will tell him that. Maybe you can tell him while you proclaim your love for his best friend. And speak to him about your quest for a child.'

She knew that it was somewhat unkind to say it

like that. But Beatrice didn't know. She was a child
about these things. She didn't understand the sort of
fate that could await a woman like Eleanor. She did
not have the protection of Hugh's name. Not really.
Not in truth.

'You know that I can't. Once something is in his
mind you cannot change it.'

She nearly laughed. 'Yes. I do know that.'

'What is between Briggs and myself is very private. I think it is love.' She did not sound pleased
about it.

But what was there to be happy about? When you
were in love and it was impossible. What was there
to be pleased about?

And maybe that was simply it. You had to stop
drifting. You had to stop surrendering to it. This thing
between herself and Hugh, it did not have to be. She
might have internally accused Beatrice of being cosseted, but Eleanor was in much the same way. She
had been at Bybee House all this time. She didn't
know other men. She could make a different choice.
She could.

'Maybe I will fall in love with someone I can have.
Maybe there will be a nice second son of an earl.'

Beatrice smiled at her, the sort of smile that was
sad and pitying and made her want to crawl beneath
the settee. 'You do not want a nice second son of an
earl.'

No. She wanted an arrogant bastard of a duke.

'No. Not because he is the second son of an earl.

Simply because I do not know how to love someone other than… Other than His Grace.'

She had never admitted such a thing out loud. It felt wrong. Illicit on her tongue. But why not? It was impossible. But she was here in Beatrice's home and she was telling Eleanor she wanted the impossible. Why should Eleanor not admit to being the same?

'Since when do you call him that?'

'I must. We are in London. And there is propriety to observe.'

'Has he scolded you? Has he put you in your place?' Beatrice went very pink when she said that.

'He is correct. We are in society and we must behave as if we are. I am not his sister.' She thought of the way they had travelled last night. She thought of all that stretched between them.

And Beatrice looked as if she wanted to say more, but didn't. Instead, she reached out and touched Eleanor's arm. 'I'm glad you're here. I only have William and Briggs to speak to and it's… I wanted someone to speak to. Really. I am sorry, I know that you are unmarried. But… Physical intimacy within marriage is wonderful.'

And she couldn't help laughing. That this miss was trying to explain to her something that her father's mistress had told her about when she was a child. 'I know about that.'

'Eleanor!'

And she realised with a certain amount of horror that Beatrice had assumed… 'I mean, I have not… I understand though.'

Beatrice suddenly looked wistful. 'I don't think he loves me. Or it's impossible to tell. He is…'

'What sort of father is he?' She thought of her own father, who had been wonderful in every way to all the women in his life.

'Lovely,' Beatrice said.

'Lovely?'

'He is. I don't know how else to say it.'

'It is hard for me to imagine him as a father. Given all I know of his reputation.' She sighed. 'I'm happy you're happy.' And she did mean that. For all that she felt jealous, she did mean that.

'I am not happy that you aren't,' Beatrice said.

'I will find a way. You know a woman such as myself… I was very lucky to have been taken in by your family. It is dishonourable of me to be so sad because I cannot have the impossible. I can no more take the stars down and hold them in my hands than I can aspire to be with your brother. My heart is foolish. I can go on loving him just fine married to another man.'

It would make no difference. Not having him was not having him.

'You would be content with that?'

'I would be resigned to it,' she said.

'What of your husband?'

'I daresay very few men expect love from their marriages.'

'I did not expect love from mine. But he is the very dearest thing in the world to me. He is so strong, so… Hard and remote. And yet I find I want to hold him in my arms and protect him from everything that has happened.'

The horrifying thing was understanding that. How badly she wished she could hold Hugh in her arms.

'Does he grieve his wife?' Beatrice might have to share Briggs with the woman he had loved first.

'No,' she said. 'He's... He is angry at his wife. Deeply and bitterly angry.'

'Oh,' she said.

'I know him better than I've ever known another person. I have let him do things that... And yet there is still so much I don't know.'

'I guess that is the fortunate thing about marriage being a lifetime.'

'Yes,' she said. 'I suppose that's true.'

'I can only hope I find that a remotely fortunate prospect when I'm faced with my own.'

'Let us hope a gallant and handsome man catches your eye tonight,' Beatrice said.

'Yes,' Eleanor said. 'Let us hope so.'

She had her doubts, however. That she would ever find anyone remotely as dashing as Hugh.

'You must let go of that. You won't find it easy. He got beneath your skin when you were too innocent to understand what you were allowing to happen. The mistake was made long ago. But you will be protected. You will be well. And you will be fine.'

And you will no longer pin your dreams on the Duke of Kendal.

Chapter Six

There was a ball tonight, and Anna had not yet arrived in London. He would have preferred to have her there to act as his partner for the evening.

To act as a barrier between himself and the marriage-minded mothers. And since he had not announced his engagement yet and would not without Anna present. Well, he would not be able to keep them at bay.

Is it marriage-minded mothers you wish to create a barrier for? Or is it Eleanor?

He ignored that. She had looked far too beautiful today. Delicate in that robin's-egg blue.

She tortured him. And he had the sense that she knew it. She was lovely. And he had the impression that she might taste like cream if he were to lick her skin.

He had never encountered a woman who tasted like cream, and he had no reason to believe that this particular one would. He simply felt it. Deep down. An ache in his groin that would not abate.

It was preposterous. He was a man of well explored appetites. He recalled well the time that he and Briggs had gone to a brothel in Paris and sampled every delight on the menu.

But she could not be found on any menu... She was far too rare.

Thoughts like that did nothing to help the situation.

And it was this that made him utterly unenthused about the task that was to follow.

They would have to make a trip to the modiste. She would need to be kitted out for the Season. The fashions from the country would not do, and he would need to have something new entirely made for her. They would not have time for something to be done up tonight, but he was certain they would find a suitable gown. They would make an appointment with the finest French seamstress on the high street. Of course, it was very likely she was not actually French, as there was a rash of faux French women who had started their lives as washer women in South London, but it did not matter. What mattered was appearances. And he would treat her as he would've done Beatrice if she were making a proper debut in society.

Yes. Like your sister. Which is why you're salivating over the thought of how her bosom will look overflowing one of those gowns...

'Please fetch Miss Jennings from wherever she has disappeared to,' he said to one of the members of staff as they walked by. And he was aware that he did not sound gracious, and yet he could not bring himself to be.

Eleanor appeared a moment later, her hair a bit askew, her expression serene. Almost sleepy.

'And where have you been?'

She rubbed a hand over her cheek. 'I was reading. I got very tired.'

She looked so dreadfully young just then. And he wanted to catch her up in his arms and wrap her in his jacket. Hold her close to his chest.

And then he wanted to peel that gown off her, and every layer beneath it until he could see every inch of her glorious body.

And then he would taste her. All that cream.

'We must go to the high street to get you fitted for a gown.'

'I have so many gowns,' she said.

'Not for the London Season. I was remiss not to bring you sooner. You are looking for a husband. And therefore you must be seen as the height of fashion. You could be diamond of the first water, Eleanor.'

Something like shock flitted through her expression. 'Then isn't it a good thing that you are to be engaged to Lady Paxton.'

Her words hit him like a closed fist to the gut. Because had they not discussed him marrying a diamond of the first water?

And it would never be her. They both knew it.

'Very convenient,' he said. 'Now, let us go.'

'It would be nice of you to give me some sort of warning. Shouldn't I dress more fashionably to go out and… Buy fashions?'

'There is no need,' he said.

'But it might be nice,' she said.

'Eleanor,' he said. 'Go and get in the carriage and stop turning everything into a three-act pantomime.'

'Your Grace,' she said with mock breathlessness. 'You are so authoritative.'

Anger flared through him, his temper getting the better of him.

He took a step towards her, his blood running hot. 'I'd show you what it is to submit to my authority, Eleanor. But I don't think you would like it. So I suggest you take yourself off to the carriage.'

Colour mounted in her cheeks, and when she scurried off to do his bidding, he had the sense that it was not because she was afraid of him.

No. Not of him.

They got into the carriage, and made the journey towards the shopping district.

He avoided it at all costs. He loathed it, in fact. He had managed to avoid it with Beatrice because of her circumstances...

It had been good to see his sister earlier, however briefly. She had mostly visited with Eleanor. Good to see Briggs as well. Nice to see that everything in the house was well ordered, and they seemed happy enough. Beatrice got to be on her little adventure without compromising her health... He could count that as one thing checked off his list.

His sister was taken care of. His ward would be next. And then he would have to see to the task of getting himself wed.

Which was where Anna came in. Anna, who did

not fire his blood, but gave him a sense of peace. She would be a fine duchess and a good mother. She was exactly the sort of woman he needed. Especially after the broken engagement.

He looked at Eleanor, and he could feel her emotions. They seemed to radiate from her.

'I'm very sorry to inconvenience you with my generosity.'

'Yes. That is what they say about you. Generous. So generous.'

'I am.'

'Truly, we should all be grateful to you. You had an ill sister, a mother who needed to be taken care of, and a ward. You are a saint, Hugh, for putting up with all the women in your life that cause you nothing but trouble. Good job you'll have shifted both myself and Beatrice before the end of the Season.'

'Come now, Eleanor, you are not settled business yet. I cannot wait until you are.'

'Shall I select a partner tonight?'

'Don't be desperate, darling. Wait a couple of balls. Won't you?'

She looked as if she wished to attack him. But that was all fine. He would prefer for there to be animosity between them. It was easier.

When the street became too crowded for the carriage to manoeuvre easily he and Eleanor got out, and he led the brisk walk down to the modiste.

'Behave yourself. Act as if you are a lady.'

'Rather than the daughter of a merchant?'

'If you must take it that way.'

She huffed and walked ahead of him but stopped at the door to the shop and let him go in first.

'Your Grace,' the woman said, practically fluttering when they entered. And he hated this sort of show. She cared not for him. Only his coin. Fine by him. But he could do without the melodrama.

'This is my ward,' he said. 'Eleanor Jennings. She needs a wardrobe for the Season. And we will require something for tonight.'

'Oh,' the modiste said. 'I fear, Your Grace, that many of the gowns made in colours more suitable for debutantes have been snapped up.'

'What have you?'

She took out a dress of midnight-blue that was too close to black for his taste. And then another in a soft, luxurious-looking fabric that made him itch to touch it. It was a dark red, that would surely not be appropriate for a debutante. And yet he knew that it would suit her perfectly.

'Try the red,' he said.

'The claret?' the modiste asked.

'I'm a duke, Madame. If I took the time to memorise all the colours, I would not have time to keep track of the management of my estate. And I think we know which is more important.'

Eleanor looked irritated by his commentary. And he was being a prick, he knew it. But that did not stop him.

But she went behind the curtain to dress, and he had to ignore—yet again—the sounds of her removing a garment.

The modiste helped her dress, and she emerged quickly. His first inclination was to tell the modiste to burn the garment, and never let any woman wear it in public, much less his ward.

For there must be something indecent about it.

The colour made her look just that much more pale, fragile. It highlighted the exquisite line of her bosom, and made his teeth ache.

'I take it His Grace approves,' the modiste said, eyeing him far too insightfully.

And he found he couldn't speak. He did not have a rejoinder. He had nothing. Nothing at all.

'Get it,' he said finally.

The rest of the trip was all spent with Eleanor selecting fabrics. And thankfully, mercifully, she removed that gown. But she would be in it tonight.

Perfect. Tonight he would look at her and that gown, a gown that made his body throb, and he would watch her dance with other men. He would watch her choose herself a husband. And then he would forget about this, this feeling, once and for all.

Chapter Seven

She felt alive in this dress. And she told herself it was because the colour was particularly flattering, and she told herself it had nothing to do with the look on Hugh's face when she had come out from behind the screen at the modiste's. She told herself that. But she knew that it wasn't strictly true. Because she had looked at his face and she had seen hunger. And it had resonated deeply inside her.

She was hungry.

Hungry for the physical intimacy that Beatrice alluded to when she spoke of herself and Briggs. Hungry for what his touch called up inside of her.

Hungry for that thing that would make you ruined.

That would make her a mistress and never a wife.

She took that and she tried to direct it elsewhere. Not at Hugh. It was difficult of course, sharing a carriage with him to the incredible city dwelling where the ball was held tonight.

But she thought of this place. This place that she

now stood in front of with him. Inside there she would find her future husband. And in this dress, she would not fail. Because she was beautiful. A diamond of the first water. And Hugh had decided that they could not be together. No. Society had decided that, long before the two of them were ever born.

It was a strange thing, her beauty. It was presented to her as fact by the people around her like they might mention her eye colour or her height. It brought her no pride, though it had initially given her a sense of relief.

Her beauty might make it easy to find a husband. To avoid becoming a mistress.

But it had never mattered, not really. Because Hugh didn't care.

Even if he could have you, you don't know that he would. Not for anything more than a plaything.

That was the other thing that Missy told her. That men liked variety. They could only take one wife, but they would like to take many mistresses. Even if Hugh did want her, did that make her anything special? Anything more than a new flavour to sample. Cherry tonight, in this gown. A momentary distraction, but nothing more.

Even without the dictates of society, perhaps Anna Paxton was his preference. Perhaps.

They walked inside, and she was immediately distracted by the glory of the place. The white marble everywhere, so splendid and bright. The candles, the sconces, they glimmered off the cream-coloured stone, and the place was like heaven.

The women looked like angels. All in sweet, pale-coloured confections. Except for her. And Beatrice.

Beatrice was also in red. Resplendent and looking very happy. And she hoped very much that Hugh did not dim that happiness. For while she had known a moment of jealousy when she had been sitting with her friend, she realised that cloistered or not, Beatrice hadn't chosen her life any more than Eleanor had. Beatrice wanted her husband to love her. She wanted a baby. She hadn't chosen her health. It was simply something that had happened to her. They were both captives of the whims of fate. And they were both in red. A surprise, to everyone, she hoped.

She separated from him as quickly as possible, there was no need to have him standing behind her like a spectre all in black. She was gathered up by a group of ladies, who made gay and lovely conversation, and she tried not to make too much of a show of scanning the ballroom. It didn't take long for her dance card to fill. There were so many men. All in variations of the same fashionable dress. Whether the breeches be black or buckskin, whether the coats be grey or a sort of soft mahogany. They were a rotation of the same sort. All pleasantly handsome in a banal sort of way. A safe way.

They were interested in her. And she much less interested in them. And it was… Utterly satisfying to realise that. Utterly and completely.

For she had spent all these years being drawn to Hugh in ways that she could not control, could not understand… And here these men were drawn to her. And she was unaffected.

She could find her way through this. She could grow to like this.

Perhaps that would be her choice. A man who was devoted to her.

And why couldn't she have that? Not a man who stood cold and aloof away from her. But a man who was desperate to be with her.

The very thought of it made her chest ache. Made her heart squeeze tight.

And she found herself looking over at Hugh. So cold and remote. Why would she consign herself to a life with a man like that?

The music began to play, and her first partner came to collect her. She went happily with him out onto the dance floor. And they stood across from one another and began the familiar movements.

And all the while she did her best not to be distracted by Hugh, who was speaking to Briggs and Beatrice. She could see when he became agitated, and she knew a moment of anxiety. She let her partner spin her, and then returned to a line of female dancers. And she looked back at the three of them, and saw that it was a fight in earnest now.

Oh, no. He must've found out about Beatrice and Briggs, and the fact that their marriage was no longer one in name only. She made the decision not to leave her partner, and when the next song started up, she simply went along with the following partner. And the next. She distanced herself from them, from Hugh. She would have to make her own life. She loved Beatrice, but she could hardly intervene in this. Hugh would only look at her with that icy glare and call her a silly virgin. She would not be allowed to speak on such matters. And really what did she know of them? She had told Beatrice that she understood intimate matters between a husband and a wife, but she knew them in blurry terms. And certainly not in the soft, satisfied way that Beatrice seemed to.

That dogged her. The idea that her friend was now more worldly than she. And she shut that out of her mind, and kept on dancing.

Until she was spun to the edge of the dance floor and came face-to-face with the Duke of Kendal. And he was a storm.

He knew that he had gone too far. But when it had become clear to him that his sister and his friend did not have the relationship that Briggs had promised him, he had pushed. He was worried for her life. For Beatrice's life, and Briggs had allowed his prick to do the thinking for him.

The bastard.

And perhaps it had been wrong of him to bring up Briggs's late wife. The manner in which she had died. But the woman had taken her own life rather than live another day with Briggs and his unusual appetites. Hugh didn't care what the man did in his bed. Until it involved his sister, and then he cared quite a lot. Briggs was a deviant. A man who liked ropes and pain, and all the things that Hugh did not wish to imagine being visited on the girl that he had spent his entire life protecting.

And now he was… Incandescent.

And when Eleanor met his eyes, and stopped at the edge of the dance floor, something hard slugged him in the stomach.

What really makes you so angry?

Worry. Worry for his sister. Obviously.

'We must go,' he said.

'I have dances yet on my card,' she said.

'Eleanor…'

'I have dances yet on my card,' she repeated. 'Your Grace.'

'And I am ready to leave.'

'You can send the carriage for me and…'

'Have you forgotten your place? Have you forgotten that you are my ward and I am the Duke? We are not equals, and you will not make suggestions to me.'

Her eyes widened. 'Will you carry me out of here then?'

'You know that I will not.'

'Then you will send a carriage, Your Grace. For I am having a wonderful time. And the fight that you are in with your best friend and your sister is not my concern. You cannot control them, any more than you can control me. I know we are all supposed to fall down to be grateful for your money and your influence. Briggs might not need it because he is a duke, but you know that Beatrice had to because she is a woman, and that I certainly have to because I am a woman of no consequence. And perhaps in the future that will have to be observed. Perhaps I will regret tonight. But just now you do not get to tell me what I will do with my evening. Goodnight, Your Grace.'

And she stepped away, back to the dance floor, back to that insolent, pale interpretation of a man that was holding her in his arms. And he knew that she had made the right decision. For he should not be alone with her.

Is that what really enrages you? That you cannot do what you want. And Briggs has done it. He doesn't care for your edicts. He cares for nothing. Not even Beatrice's own good. So what holds you back?

Nothing. Not any more. He would go to a brothel, which he had sworn he was done with, but this was a matter of emergent need. And he would find a woman upon whom he could unleash this thing. And have it done. A beautiful blonde who liked his brand of play, and he would have her put on a crimson gown. And he would tear it from her body. And he would lay her down and he would lick her from her ankle all the way up to that place between her thighs. But she would not taste like cream. And she would not be Eleanor. But he could be rough with her. He could leave bruises on that pale skin. Just as he liked.

You know better than Briggs. But you can hardly claim that you're different.

No. He would not go to a brothel. He would draft a letter to Anna, so that she might meet him tomorrow. And then he would state his intentions. Tomorrow, he would get engaged. And that would make all of this go away.

Chapter Eight

Well. She had done it. She had basically told Hugh to sod off in no uncertain terms, which was maybe not the best thing to say to a duke who was also your guardian. But she wanted to stay. She wanted… She wanted something. Anything. And these men that were flitting around her like she was something magical meant something.

So she stayed and she danced, even longer than Bea and Briggs remained, which had been foolish, and then she went outside, hoping there was a carriage for her, because Hugh had been awfully angry. But of course, he would never leave her without a way to get home, evidenced by the fact that a carriage was there when she went to leave.

By the time she got home, he would likely be up in his study, having an angry brandy.

She leaned back in the carriage, and was distressed to discover that she missed his imposing presence.

Why? Why should she miss him at all? The men

that she had danced with tonight were lovely. And they approved of her. They didn't act as if touching her was a violation. Of themselves.

It was easy and it was lovely. And it didn't hurt. And she should be glad of that.

Instead, she missed him, and she was bored, the whole carriage ride home.

When they pulled up to the front of the town house and she was helped from the carriage, she looked up at the windows and wondered if he was still awake.

She shouldn't want him to be. She shouldn't want to see him. He had been an absolute ogre to Briggs and Beatrice, and she didn't need to hear what he'd said to know that.

She should wish to avoid him at all costs.

She went inside, and found that he was nowhere to be seen. The maids appeared to help with her cloak, her gloves. And then she went upstairs, towards her room. Except she found herself headed towards his study. She was supposed to leave him to his rage. Leave him to his study. She was supposed to want nothing to do with either. And yet there she was, headed in his direction.

Her heart was pounding so hard it made her feel ill.

She didn't know why.

But she did.

She was baiting him. Looking for a fight, because a fight was the closest thing she could have to what she truly wanted with him. It was the closest thing to losing control. The closest thing to a lack of civility that she ever saw in him.

She wanted it. She craved it. The way that she could push him over the edge. The way his face would turn to stone, and he would issue threats about bringing her to heel.

It was when she saw that no matter how hard he tried, he was not the man that he pretended to be. He was not half so civilised. Not half so upstanding.

And she knew that. Only she.

It made her giddy with something bright and reckless.

She didn't knock. She opened the door. And there he was, leaning against his desk, his shirtsleeves pushed up past his elbows, his hair dishevelled.

'What are you doing here?'

'I thought that you would wish to know that I had arrived back safely.'

'So you have.'

He raised his glass as if to her, and then took a drink.

'What did you fight about with Briggs?' As if she didn't already know.

'Nothing that is fit for your ears to hear.'

Exactly as she had thought. He was going to dismiss her. Treat her like an innocent.

'Ah. The fact that he has made your sister his wife. In truth.'

She stood there and watched the words hit, and for a moment it was utterly satisfying.

And then he stood, the rage emanating from him taking on a life of its own.

'What do you know about that?'

'What do I know about a man and a wife? Or about this particular one?'

'You speak of that which you should not.'

'Why? Why all these… These games?' And suddenly she knew it all. Because everything in this world, in this society, was a game about what a woman could and could not know, while that very thing determined her fate. And she was so… So viscerally aware of it. And everyone around you acted as if it wasn't happening.

'Do you expect me to not know, Hugh? That it is the very thing that could lower me for the rest of my life. And here we are, supposed to be innocent flowers about it all. I am not Beatrice. I am not a lady. My father had a mistress, and she told me what would happen to me if I made a mistake. What I would become. I was never afforded the chance to be a real innocent. Not when the stakes were so high. Do not speak to me as if I'm nothing more than a silly virgin. I am a fearsome virgin, who has done all she can to ensure that she does not squander what she has been given, while her body demands satisfaction. Do not speak to me as if I don't understand.'

And she turned to walk away, but he nearly leapt across his desk and grabbed her arm. 'And what is it that tempts you?'

'Oh, don't ask me that now. I will not give you the satisfaction.'

'What tempts you?' he asked, reaching out and grabbing hold of her chin. Her pulse fluttered so hard she could scarcely breathe.

'All of those lovely men at the ball tonight. I cannot get enough of such attention. Why, if one of them had asked me to the garden, or to a game of charades, I would've lifted my skirts in an instant.'

'Lies. You had better lie.'

'Do you not know?' she asked, edging close. Far too close to the truth of it all.

'Provocative minx.'

'And why not? Why not see how hard I can push you? How far? You are so proud of yourself, Hugh. So certain that you're better than your father, than Briggs. Are you? You get so angry when you see me with men, and yet you lack the spine to do anything about it.'

'I lack the dishonour to sully you when as you said, you must remain pure.'

'And is it a trial?'

She waited, her breath frozen in her lungs, for the admission of what she hoped. What she'd thought she'd glimpsed in those moments of fire between them.

'You're beautiful,' he said.

Beautiful.

Beautiful.

For the first time the word didn't feel like nothing. For the first time it made her feel cherished.

For the first time, it mattered.

But then he continued. 'There is not a man in England who wouldn't take the free and easy chance to rut between your thighs. I among them. But that's all. That's all it would be.'

His coarse words sent a shiver down her spine. He was being awful. He was being awful on purpose. And perhaps she would join him. Down here. Where there was no civility at all. Where there was nothing but rage.

'How do you know I wouldn't say yes?' She stared at him, watching his face. 'But you're very honourable, aren't you? I'm certain that if you had a taste, you would be able to stop.'

And that was when she found herself being hauled over the desk, and brought down to his side, his arm around her like a vice, his hand on her chin, uncompromising. He brought his face down, a breath from hers, and she found herself drifting up towards him.

'Do you want to know the real truth? I would have no trouble stopping,' he said, letting his mouth hover over hers, a delicious temptation that she wanted to go on for ever, and that she also needed to end. This torture. Such torture. 'Because I'm not even tempted to begin.'

He released his hold on her, and she felt cold, frozen. And then he turned, and walked out of the study, leaving her feeling as if he had stripped her bare and seen all the deepest, darkest desires inside her, only to utterly destroy them. Leaving them tattered at her feet. Along with her pride.

Chapter Nine

It was done. He had visited Anna at the town house her late husband's family allowed her to live in and asked for her hand. She had accepted, he had kissed her hand. He had left.

He could sense her disappointment, with the tepid kiss, but he simply didn't have it in him. Not while Eleanor burned in his blood.

Damn her.

She knew. Except she did not know.

He would be able to control himself with Anna. They would have a nice union. Bedding her would be no hardship.

It was Eleanor who created this uncontrollable fire in him. Eleanor who made it all impossible.

Even if she were not his ward, she was not the woman he would choose.

Control was everything. The fact that he had sent her away last night was a testament to his.

He had felt her burning in his arms. But she did

not really know what she asked. She could not. She was far too innocent. And yet in his arms she had not felt so. She had felt passionate.

And he had rebuffed her. Now he was engaged. Tonight they would make their debut as a couple. And today the first of Eleanor's dresses would be delivered. And he would not think of how she might look in it.

Just as he would not think of Briggs and his sister.

Dammit all. He found himself not going home. Rather, he went to the home of a physician that he had known for a great many years. Not the one who had cared for Beatrice when she was a girl, but a different man.

'And I know that you did not treat her as a child, but what are your thoughts on her having children of her own?'

The doctor, a man about his age, leaned back in his chair. 'Childbirth is a dangerous business,' he said. 'I cannot guarantee that any woman will make it through. However, it does not sound to me that your sister is in any greater danger than another woman might be.'

'But she was an incredibly sickly child.'

'Understandable. But it sounds as if adulthood has evened out her constitution, which is quite common. Breathing maladies can persist while a person is still developing maturity. And sometimes exercise and other things can strengthen the constitution.'

'My sister has never done… Exercise.'

'You say she seems hale and hearty now. Perhaps you should speak to her.'

A novel concept. Speaking to his sister.

'But you honestly think that… That she can…'

'Like I said. The business of birthing children is a dangerous one, but many women do just fine with it. If they didn't, the world would be a much darker place, wouldn't it?'

'I don't know that I should trust you, Hawkins, I've seen you at the backgammon table.'

'Well, you do not need to trust me. You are a duke, and I a physician. Society would say that you are much smarter than I. Though, my training suggests that perhaps I know a bit more about medical related issues than you. And you did come to speak to me.'

'Yes,' he said. 'I did.'

'Just consider the possibility that your sister will be just fine. Consider the life that she could have. It sounds to me like she survived a rather harrowing childhood. It would be a shame for her to have survived that and to needlessly deny herself such a great joy in this life. She is married, I assume?'

'Yes. She is.'

'You will always worry about those you love. I cannot say that being a physician has eased my thoughts when it comes to those I care for. I have seen the most common and easy outcomes, and the grimmest of complications play out across all manner of situations. It is part of being a doctor. But if she were my sister, I would let go. Allow her to have her life. To have her happiness.'

'Thank you.'

So now he was engaged, and quite possibly in the wrong when it came to his dealings with Briggs and Beatrice. His sister had said that she enjoyed the sorts of things that Briggs did, and that was something he could've gone his entire life without being aware of.

You inserted yourself into their affairs, and now you're angry for being told of them.

He disliked the fact that his internal compass did not seem to be working in his favour.

Then there was the matter of Eleanor...

The truth was, it was perhaps easier to worry about Briggs and Bea than the way Eleanor made him feel.

When he arrived back in his town house, there was a delivery of two trunks being made.

'What is all this?' he asked the porters.

'Dresses for Miss Jennings.'

'I was only expecting one today.'

'Madame Bouvier had her seamstresses work overnight to alter a few pieces that were in stock. The rest will come within a fortnight.'

'Thank her for me.'

He had a feeling that Eleanor had been gifted someone else's trousseau, likely because he was a duke. And without pre-agreeing on a price, he would pay handsomely for it, and she knew it.

It was true, Eleanor benefited greatly from her association with him. And she was exceedingly ungrateful. He asked two of the manservants to take the trunks upstairs to Eleanor's chambers, and he went to his study. And unfortunately, the study was... Imbued with her presence. He could not ignore what had occurred there last night. He could not forget it. But there was some perverse sort of satisfaction from knowing he had not acted on it. That he had not taken her up on what she was offering.

The day went by quickly, and he knew that he faced yet another ball. But this time they would be picking up Anna on the way. Perhaps he should send an entirely separate carriage for Eleanor, to draw a line underneath their association. He would. He left the house without seeing her even once the entire day. He instructed his staff to send her in her own carriage.

He went straight in his own carriage to Anna's house. She looked lovely, in a navy-blue gown befitting her status. She looked mature, and beautiful all at once. Not the lovely debutante that Eleanor was, but he did not require that.

She was a woman with gravitas, and that was exactly what he needed.

Eleanor carries her own sort of weight.

He shoved that thought aside, and yet the impression of her remained. Validating that thought.

He didn't care.

Tonight they would announce their engagement at the ball, and by morning it would be written up in the scandal sheets and society news for all to see. A fitting duchess for the Duke, wholly different to the woman who had left him in the lurch nearly a year before.

'Your Grace,' she said, lowering her eyes for a moment before looking back up at him and smiling. She was definitely making it known that she was open to some further physical attentions than he'd given her as yet. It irked him, and it shouldn't. She had been married before. There was no reason for them not to test their attraction to one another.

Your issue is that you're not attracted to her.

He was attracted enough.

'You look beautiful,' he said, kissing her knuckles as he helped her into the carriage.

'Miss Jennings is not joining us tonight?'

'Miss Jennings will be at the ball. She will attend with my sister.'

'Of course.'

But she looked at him in a strange sort of way and it made him want to justify himself. To make it clear what Eleanor's position was. He had not thought that Anna believed there was anything untoward between himself and Eleanor, but her expression did make him wonder. But he would not explain himself. He would not start this relationship off that way.

He owed no one any explanations for who he was. He had proved himself to be everything his father had never been.

He had not earned anyone's suspicions.

The party was being held at one of the grandest estates in all of London. An exceedingly rich merchant who had amassed wealth that far outstripped most of the nobility in the country. And he paid handsomely to have them attend his parties. Paid handsomely for this position in society.

It was the perfect venue for him to announce his engagement.

When he and Anna entered the room, he informed them that they were to be announced as the Duke and future Duchess of Kendal.

As they were, a ripple went through the crowd, and scanning that crowd, he saw Eleanor. Her arm linked with a gentleman—the Earl of Something or Another—and he saw her face go pale.

She did not shrink away, did not make an emotional show of anything. Along with everyone else, she turned and went back to the dance.

But his eyes lingered on her. On the pale pink gown that she wore, much more fitting for a debutante than the red she had worn the previous night.

But he had loved the red.

He had no business loving the red.

They were swept up in attention after that. Women fawning over Anna as if they had always been her dearest friends.

It made his lip curl. He had to participate in such things because it was how the world ran, but he found them disingenuous and false.

If Anna was bothered by it, it was impossible to tell. It was exactly why she was so perfect. She was unreadable. Utterly and completely. No one would ever know what she thought of anything. She had a feline sort of smile, and a vague manner. But it always seemed unfailingly polite and gracious. Her true feelings would only be known if she wished to share them, and she was the sort of woman who seemed happy to not share. Who seemed perfectly content to be a mystery.

His eyes should be on her. But they weren't. His eyes were continually searching for Eleanor.

'Do you not dance?' Anna asked as the night wore on.

'Of course I do. My apologies. I have been remiss. I should've asked if you wish to dance.'

'I haven't in a very long time.' She looked at him, her grey eyes very serious. 'I would like to, Your Grace. I would like to dance again.'

There was a weight to those words. She didn't want to mourn. She wanted a life. And she was asking him if he could give her that. Life.

And so he took her out to the dance floor, and put his own rather unused dance skills to the test.

Eleanor was with a different partner to the one that she had danced with previously. The man was clearly besotted with her. Utterly and completely.

He couldn't blame him. Her cheeks were pinker than the dress she wore, flushed with exertion from dancing. And he could not help but think she would be flushed like that in his bed.

With pleasure.

He gritted his teeth and turned away.

'Is all well, Your Grace?' Anna asked.

'All is well,' he said, forcing a smile. 'All is well indeed. You have nothing to be concerned about.'

They danced for two songs, and then went back for punch and more socialising. He noticed that Briggs and Bea were not in attendance, and he knew that was his fault. And somehow, even with Beatrice taken care of, even with Eleanor well on her way to an engagement, he felt as if he had somehow made a hash of everything. And he was not accustomed to that sensation.

Eleanor's dance partner whispered something in her ear, and she looked as if she was considering it. Then nodded in the affirmative. The man walked away from the dance floor, as did Eleanor, and Hugh's senses twitched.

'Would you like some ratafia?' he asked Anna.

'I think if I have any more I might float away. Or lose my senses.'

'I would like some. If we separate for a moment, will the hounds consume you?'

'I assume you mean the ladies. And I do not fear them. Silly girls filled with petty jealousies. But they will be kind to me because I'm to be a duchess. I'm not a fool. I know exactly why they deigned to speak to me.'

He looked at her face and noticed lines of resignation there. 'You are a lady in your own right.'

'But a widow. And everyone secretly fears that widows will rub their bad luck off on to them, don't you think?'

'I don't. I don't see your being a widow as a detraction.'

'No,' she said. 'You are very… Practical, aren't you?'

She said that as if it were somewhat sad.

'I thought that you were as well. A woman of great practicality and propriety.'

'Because I must be. But that does not mean there is not more. Is there any more to you, Your Grace?'

He looked past her to Eleanor, who was now rushing to the back of the ballroom, slipping outside.

Dammit all.

'No,' he said, his voice hard. 'There is not. But if you will excuse me, I have to intervene in a situation.'

She looked at him, as if she knew things that he did not, and he did not care for it.

'Do what you must. And as I said, out of necessity, I am a woman of great practicality.'

But he did not think too long on what that might mean, because he was already halfway across the ballroom, headed out through the door where Eleanor had just escaped.

She was going out to the garden with that scoundrel. They had obviously agreed to exit separately. And he would be damned. He would be damned if some bounder took her innocence, or compromised her in any way. She had the full array of choice before her of men to marry, and a man whose name Hugh could not even readily produce in his mind was not good enough for her.

He left behind everything. His new fiancée, and the thought of punch, and his ability to maintain calm. He wove through the crowd of people and went right out that same door. The night air was cool, crisp.

And he saw the edge of her pink gown disappear into the hedge.

This was no mistake. No misunderstanding. This was not a game of charades.

And she did not know better. She had been pushing and pushing, and now she was playing with fire in a much more serious fashion than she had even with him.

She would be burned. And he would be damned.

He went into the hedge, and she disappeared around the corner. What the hell was the fascination with mazes in gardens? It was as if the entire point of them was for carnal assignations. He imagined that was the entire point of them. He would never have a maze at any of his residences. He imagined Briggs had several. Several that he made use of with Hugh's sister. And now his ward was out in one.

Damn.

He rounded the corner, and saw Eleanor standing there, looking from her left to her right. Then she saw him and her eyes went wide.

'You are not half so sneaky as you seem to think.'

'What are you doing out here?'

'I followed you, because I had the good sense to know that you were headed into trouble.'

'You should be with your fiancée.'

'You should not presume to tell me what to do.'

'Perhaps not. But then… I'm not sure why you're so concerned with me.'

'You are my ward,' he said.

'And we are out in the garden together.'

He cursed, low and sharp, and grabbed her arm, dragging her into an alcove off the main path that was well concealed. 'Hopefully this is not where your would-be lover was going to meet you.'

'He was not going to be my… It was only going to be… I was only going to meet him for a kiss.'

'Any deeper into the garden and you're not asking for a kiss, my sweet girl.'

She stared up at him, her eyes bright. Dangerous. 'And what am I asking for?'

Heat flared in his gut. Reckless. Heedless. All things he was not. Ever. Except when faced with Eleanor. And he loved it when he was angry with her because wasn't the anger better? Simpler?

Wasn't it the best and safest way to feel with her? Anything else…

Anything else would be unthinkable.

'Right now? You are asking for punishment. You are certainly asking for a firm hand as you cannot seem to manage yourself on your own.'

He hated himself for that. Because while she might not be able to see inside his mind, he could see his own desires all too well. The kind of authority he wished to exert over her had nothing to do with a parental or brotherly sort of guidance.

He would see her stripped bare. Her hands and feet bound, her body offered up to him in supplication as he instructed her on exactly where her desires could lead her.

'So wise, Hugh, and yet here you are in the middle of the garden with me rather than inside with your new fiancée. Were you going to tell me? Or was this your plan? To ambush me with the news?'

'You shouldn't care,' he said.

'No,' she said, her voice low and fierce, making

his stomach tighten. 'I should not care. Nothing in me should give a damn about any of this. Because you certainly don't give a damn about me.' She shook her head. 'Except here you are, interfering. Why can I not have a kiss? Why can I not live? I'm not Beatrice.'

No, a kiss might not put her health in danger, but it would put her in a precarious situation in every other way.

He gritted his teeth. 'You must have a care for your reputation.'

He could see, by the fire in her eyes, that she knew that well. But she was choosing to fight, not engage in reason. 'Well maybe I'm going to marry him.'

'Has he offered? Because you must remember your position, Eleanor. You are not a lady. If the man has not offered, and yet has asked you for a rendezvous in the garden, he may have no designs on you whatsoever other than an intent on possessing your body. And what then? When he tells all of his snickering friends that he's had you? Who do you think will have you then? Who do you think will marry you? You are so concerned about becoming a mistress and yet you are behaving recklessly.'

'You're right,' she said, looking shocked. 'You're right. I am behaving recklessly. And if I am going to behave recklessly then it ought to be to get what I actually want.' She laughed. 'If I'm going to lose everything... I should really try to lose everything.'

And before he could ask what she meant, she drew closer to him, her scent intoxicating, and he remembered that scent from last night. The way he had taken her into his arms before cruelly rebuffing her.

And he had been cruel. More, he had been a liar. An outright liar. And she looked so beautiful in this dress. So innocent. Like everything she was. Young and pretty and forbidden. And he craved her. He did not crave practical, lovely Anna. And he should. By all rights he should. But this was the one perversion that he could not seem to master. This desperate need for his ward.

And this piece of him was his father's, and he knew it well.

She wouldn't do it. She wouldn't close the distance between them, because she was too innocent. Because she didn't know how to do it. So it was up to him. Up to him to destroy all that he had built with one touch of his mouth to hers.

And in a breath, the decision was made.

He caught her up in his arms, and he lowered his head and crashed his lips against hers.

Chapter Ten

It was happening. Hugh was kissing her. She had never been kissed before. And it was… It was a fire. A raging inferno that started in her belly and spread everywhere. The heat it generated between her thighs was unbearable. It was instantaneous, and it was deadly. And she ached with it. Ached for him.

She wrapped her arms around his neck. He was so strong. The way the solid wall of muscle that was his chest pressed against her breasts, made her so aware of his size, his strength, the way that she was able to cling to him… He was her dearest held fantasy, and she had no idea. No real idea of what it would mean when his lips touched hers. Not really.

Hugh.

Not His Grace. But Hugh.

Her endless, undying fantasy. And how foolish she'd been. She'd told Beatrice that she knew all about intimacy, but she had not even known about *a kiss*.

The heat of a man's mouth, of his body pressed against hers.

And when he tilted his head and fitted his mouth more firmly against hers, parted his lips and swept his tongue against hers, she was undone. She truly had not known.

She gasped, and it allowed him deeper entry to her mouth. The slick friction of his tongue against hers made an echoing desire move through her core, and she felt a shameful heat between her legs. How did he affect her there…? How? She didn't understand.

This was desire. Real desire. Like a fever, like a sickness. She hurt. Hurt for more of his touch, and her gown felt far too tight, like it was keeping her from all that was good and wonderful. Like it was keeping her from him. She wanted nothing between them.

She wanted to be naked with him. His skin against hers. And the very idea made her body ripple with need.

'Hugh,' she sobbed, and he pressed his hand to the back of her head and only kissed her harder, kept her from speaking again. As if he couldn't bear it. While she couldn't bear it either. Not any of this. This desire, this need, this brokenness over the fact that he was engaged.

She moved her hands through his hair. His hair. That beautiful, golden hair that she loved so much. And she was touching it. Touching him. It made her want to weep.

He was so familiar. She had spent years looking at him, nearly every day for all of these years, but she had not touched him. Not beyond the simple brush of her fingertips against his arm, his gloved hand against hers.

Now her fingers were in his hair. His tongue was in her mouth. And it wasn't enough. Perhaps it would never be enough.

Blessed and damn, what if it was never enough? What if this ache lived in her for ever? What if she was never free of it?

She had no answers to that, so she kissed him. Luxuriating in the sensation. She moved her hands down the back of his neck, felt the heat of his skin, before skimming them over his broad shoulders. Down his back, then up again and down his chest. Covered though it was by his jacket, she could still feel his heat. His hardened muscles beneath. He was so strong. He did not have the physique of most men in the upper classes. Hugh was a man who worked. A man who took care to treat his body as if it were a temple.

And it was one she wished to worship at more than anything. Perhaps that was a blasphemy but she couldn't bring herself to care because she was lost in this. In him. In the truth of the knowledge that if she were to be ruined, this was the only way to be ruined. In his arms.

His hands had been still, one on the back of her head, the other planted between her shoulder blades, but then they began to move, down her back, around to the front of her bodice, his thumbs just beneath her breasts. And when he moved his hands upward to capture the needy globes in his hands, she gasped. It was such a base thing. Animalistic. Something she had never imagined. And he was doing it. To her. Controlled, perfect Hugh had his hands on her breasts. And then he moved his thumbs over the stinging points, aching and needy even through the fabric of her gown, and she gasped at the sensation.

'Please,' she whispered.

And suddenly they heard voices. He broke away from her with speed, and she was left standing there, breathing hard, cold. Bereft of his touch.

'Enough.'

He looked dishevelled. Even in the dim light of the garden she could see that the colour in his cheeks was high.

'Hugh…'

'Go back to the ballroom.'

She herself must look a disaster. There was no way they were going to walk back into the ball and have people not know. She was certain that she wore it as an emblem on her skin. Desire. Her mouth felt swollen, and she could not imagine it didn't look so.

'I doubt that is a very good idea,' she said.

'No,' he said. 'You look like you've been tupped.'

She winced, his crude words making her ache.

'Don't go into the ballroom. There is likely another door you can access. But I do not wish to leave you out here where any bounder could find you.'

'Do you mean you?'

'Perhaps.' He breathed out. 'Go in the back door, linger for a while. Find a privy and stay there until you no longer look heated.'

'And what about you?'

'I will be fine by the time I walk back inside.'

Of course. Of course he would. Because this was just one of many kisses he'd had, and this was her first.

'I thought you were not tempted to start, Your Grace,' she said, because she had to do something to salvage her pride in the middle of all this.

'Congratulations,' he said. 'You've made fools of us both. And what have you accomplished?'

'I know,' she said, conviction making her voice shake. 'I know I'm not alone. And that… That will keep me warm, Your Grace. Perhaps that is accomplishment enough for a woman who is not really a lady. Perhaps it is accomplishment enough for me.'

She turned on her heel and ran blindly back through the maze, her heart pounding hard. Someone might see her, she didn't care. She didn't.

But by the time she found her way to another entrance into the house, she very much did care. Her breath was coming in hard, sharp bursts, her body trembling all over.

She did not wish to be caught. They couldn't be caught.

The very idea nearly made her…

Her shoulders heaved. She slipped into an alcove. It was dark at this end of the house, thankfully. There was no one milling around. There was nothing.

She was safe.

She'd nearly made a very costly mistake. She had a man who wanted her, and who could marry her and what had she done? She'd let her anger make her reckless.

She'd forgotten herself.

Or perhaps, for the first time she'd let her guard down and had become wholly herself. And she knew...she knew she couldn't do that. There was no room in this world for a woman such as her to do that. To want more. To demand more.

She had to accept what she was allowed, for there could be no more.

It could never happen again.

Not ever.

She would take that moment and she would lock it away tight inside herself. She would take it out only when she was alone and sometimes, she would dream of it. She would dream of him.

But only then.

She would never, ever touch him again.

He was marrying another woman.

She was going to marry another man.

She had to.

She waited several breaths. Waited until she could breathe again. And when she went back to the ball-room, the Earl of Graystone was there, obviously confused that he had not been able to find her. And Hugh was there, standing with Anna. As if nothing had happened at all.

But she knew now. She did. For all that it meant, she knew. He was not immune to her. He wanted her. He could say whatever he pleased about it, but the evidence was undeniable. He wanted her.

For all the good that it did.

She knew it now, and she could do nothing with it. Not even dream.

She was not a girl, not any more.

She was a woman, and she had to look at life practically.

Chapter Eleven

He was not a man who took any sort of transgression lightly. Not against himself, not against others. Particularly not against a friend. And after last night… There was nothing he could say to Briggs. The only thing that had stopped him from stripping Eleanor free of her gown was the fact they'd been in the garden.

If they had been back at the town house, she would've been naked and beneath him in short order.

It was the very thing that made her unsuitable that aroused him so, he told himself now. She was soft. She was fragile. And he loved the feeling of a delicate woman beneath his hands. Loved knowing just how rough he could be, just how far he could push. He would never break a woman, not ever. He only took them both to the edge so they might lose themselves utterly.

And Eleanor…

She was the epitome of that fantasy. But she was

dangerous, for her fragility was real. She was beneath his protection, which as a game would be compelling. Arousing. In reality...

It made it all impossible.

The way he'd turned her away that night in his study, killed the heat between them with a few carefully chosen words of cruelty.

But last night he hadn't. The fact that he had not deflowered her meant nothing. Nothing in context with the fact of where he was, and what he would have done had they been anywhere else.

And so now he stood in front of Briggs's town house, knowing that he had to apologise.

As if you don't owe Anna an apology.

He was a duke. And while he saw his title as a responsibility and not a license to do whatever he wished, the fact remained a certain status came with it. He did not owe her an apology for that which he did in private. As long as he did not embarrass her. And he had not. And once they said their vows to each other he would never...

Would you not? Are you in fact your father after all?

Perhaps he was.

And again the idea of going to a brothel and letting it all burn itched at the back of his mind. That night when he'd been with Eleanor in his study he'd got engaged instead. Tonight...

Perhaps tonight he would indulge himself.

He was clearly on edge. He could not justify the

way he'd behaved, not in any fashion. So maybe the time for justification was done.

Maybe it was simply time to admit that he had an unforgivable weakness in him. And the only thing to be done was to try and take the edge off this unbearable ache, with the sort of woman who would see it as it was. A business transaction. An evening for him to lose himself in sin, vice and fantasy.

She would be all right that it was not her face he saw when he entered her body.

She would not care that it was Eleanor he thought of as he kissed her, licked her.

He would not do that to Anna.

He would burn it out of him before he ever went to her bed.

What a neat justification you've made for yourself. One that means you get to find your own pleasure as soon as possible...

He was uninterested in taking jabs from himself and he schooled his mind into a blank slate during the carriage ride to the brothel.

It was a brothel he was familiar with, though it had been some time since he'd made a pilgrimage there.

But it was the sort of place where a man could indulge a myriad of fantasies, and the girls there had no issues with his unrestrained tastes. Hell, they catered to Briggs in this place. His own penchant for a little bit of roughness barely caused a ripple of reaction.

He expected his tension to ease the moment he walked in, but he found it did not.

And when he saw his friend, who was now his

brother-in-law, sitting in the lounge area of the brothel, drinking, Hugh nearly choked on his rage.

How dare he betray Beatrice like this?

After you made him feel like a monster for touching her?

It mattered not. She was his wife, and he was here in a brothel. It could not be tolerated.

It was a relief. To see Briggs here. To be so angry with him.

How badly he could use a bit of violence.

'And what the hell are you doing here?'

Briggs looked up at him, an unfocused expression in his eyes. 'Leaving your sister alone, is that not what you want?'

It was what he'd wanted, dammit. But now he knew…

Now he knew it was possible for her to have a child. Maybe.

With no guarantees.

Now he knew that…

Briggs cared for her. He could see it. Right then and there he could see it in the utter tragedy of the other man's expression.

But he was making a hash of things. Hugh was personally failing every woman in his life at the moment and even he could see that Briggs was dire.

'Like hell,' Hugh said. 'You bastard.' That he added for good measure. 'I do not want you betraying my sister. That is certain.'

'A betrayal is it?' Briggs asked. 'How is it a betrayal if she is to be my ward?'

That word dug under Hugh's skin. 'And have you

taken her innocence?' Briggs's only response was to take another drink. 'You have. Wonderful.'

'What I have or haven't done is hardly your business. You must leave me to sort out the affairs of my marriage. After all, you will wash your hands of me.' He sounded maudlin and so deep in his cups he barely made sense.

'It is only out of concern for Beatrice.' Concern was too mild a word. The fear he felt for his sister, the fear he'd always felt for her, the way he cared about her...

Their own father had been so consumed by his petty pursuits of pleasure that he'd never cared for his sickly daughter in the way he should have.

It was Hugh who had fetched physicians when they were needed. Hugh who had stood outside her bedroom door at night, listening to see if she was still breathing.

Hugh who had gone to darkened rooms and put his hand over his mouth to stifle the sounds of terror that threatened to escape on nights when the physicians did not think she would live to see the dawn.

He had worried over Beatrice all her life.

He had taken on the fear his father was too selfish to feel. That his mother was often too withdrawn to feel. He had taken everything onto his shoulders because his father had not.

Everything.

'Do you want to know a cruel joke?' Briggs asked. 'Your sister thinks that she is in love with me.'

Everything in him stopped. 'Does she?'

'Yes, she gave quite an impassioned speech to that effect.'

'And now you're here. Drunk. Why is that?' He couldn't fathom it. Not if Beatrice loved him. Hugh knew why he wanted to be drunk in a brothel, just not why Briggs wanted to be.

'Because you're right. There was no way she could possibly love me. How could she love me? How? How could she love me? I am debauched in every way. I am wrong. And I always have been. You helped me become the thing that people could tolerate. You helped turn me into a man who could at least walk into a room and have a conversation. One that was not about orchids. You took me to the brothel in Paris, and I found women there who enjoyed my particular vices. And with the exception of my late wife, with whom I made a terrible error in judgement, I have kept it there.'

He grimaced, and then he continued. 'Until Beatrice.' Hugh's stomach went tight. 'And she thinks... She thinks that she loves me for it. For all that I am. For the orchids and everything else. How is that possible? And when will it end? Because it will end. It will have to end.'

God in heaven.

They were in love.

He would never, ever have thought that Beatrice might be the fitting edge to the jagged pieces that made up his friend and yet...

He believed what Briggs said.

Perhaps there was no way to guarantee Beatrice's

safety. But could he possibly condemn her to a life of unhappiness?

She can try to claim what she wants.

It's more than you can do.

How can you do anything but support her in that?

'I have little desire to think about the ways in which you connect with my sister.' He knew too much about how Briggs enjoyed wielding a riding crop. 'However, if she says that she loves you…'

'What?' Briggs asked, his tone sardonic. 'Now you believe it might be so.'

Hugh grimaced. 'You do not have a sister, so you are forgiven for not understanding why it was not something I wish to think about. The two of you together. I know too much about you. The hazard of being friends for as long as we have been. We are now men who might deal in a bit more discretion. Whereas when we were boys, trying to figure out life's great mysteries, we were a bit more free.'

He had taken Briggs to the brothel with the menu, after all. And he'd seen what his friend had chosen. And had heard him recount it all later.

As much as Hugh didn't want to remember his own seventeen-year-old enthusiasm, he'd likely done the same.

'That is true. I'd…'

'It is not that I didn't think my sister could love you. It is that… You were right. I'm used to thinking of her as a child. I'm used to protecting her.' At all costs. With all that he was. 'Our father did nothing for us. She was merely a means for him to bring young women into the house under the guise of being her governess. He paid exorbitant fees to physicians to keep her alive. That is all true. But he loved no one beyond himself.'

If Hugh had not arranged for the physicians to come, he didn't know if Beatrice would have lived at all. It had been his father's money, but not his father's concern.

'And you have carried all of it.'

He could see that Briggs did understand.

'I have carried all of it.' He thought back to what he'd said about Briggs's first wife. He never should have. No matter his anger, he had no excuse for being that cruel. 'What I said about Serena was not fair.'

Briggs looked bleak. 'It was something I had not told her.'

Guilt, so familiar to him now, ate at him. 'Go home. You don't wish to be here.'

'I don't know where else to go.'

Hugh arched a brow. 'You will not betray my sister.'

Briggs shook his head. 'No. Do you know, when we went to the brothel it was revolutionary for me? Because it was easy. I risked nothing to explore what I desired. It was a transaction.' The words were so close to the bone of what Hugh was doing here that it stung. 'I have always found those things much easier than real life. But they do not last.'

'These things are not real,' he said, his own vision of finding a woman to stand in for Eleanor curling into smoke and blowing away on the wind. 'You cannot take them with you into your life. The women here…they don't know you.'

Eleanor knew him.

Eleanor had made him a cake.

Eleanor had seen even then that the world was on his shoulders and sometimes…

Sometimes he was tired.

'Don't you see?' Briggs asked, his lips curved into a rueful smile. 'I consider that a good thing.'

Briggs was not one of Hugh's responsibilities, and he never had been. But he wondered if his friend knew that. He had never considered it. Briggs had had a terrible time fitting in at school. When they were young he'd had strange mannerisms. Trouble meeting people's eyes. He didn't do a better job with that last bit now, but it seemed aloof on a duke in his thirties, not strange as it had on a teenage boy.

Then there was his obsession with flowers. His dominant streak when it came to lovers.

He wasn't like anyone else Hugh knew.

But he'd always liked him for it. Not in spite of it.

'Briggs, I never liked you for what you pretended to be. I of all people know exactly where you come from. Exactly who you are. Do you not know that?'

'It feels to me…'

'And if I did anything to harm the relationship between you and my sister, I am sorry. I handled it badly.' He was not given to apologies.

A shame he'd found himself in need of making so many lately.

'Does this have something to do with Eleanor?'

He could hardly breathe around that question. And of course, leave it to Briggs to make eye contact now. 'I am everything my father was not.' He said it as a vow to himself. 'And that is my deepest source of pride in this life.'

'But it is not an answer.'

'It is the only answer I can give. Beatrice married you. She has taken you every way that you come. And she has said that she loved you first. If you cannot even be half as brave as my sister... Then perhaps you are not the man I thought you were.'

He turned away from Briggs then, and began to walk up the stairs. Still intent on his mission to find a woman.

He was not his father.

He would not be his father.

He had given Briggs his blessing and he better bloody well go make things right with Beatrice.

He would not stand in the way of his friend. And he would not see that relationship destroyed. Not now. Not when he cared about Beatrice so much. Not when he cared about Briggs as he did.

His friend. It was as if now he had to reach out to him, even more than ever before, because...

There had been a time when he'd taught Briggs what it was to be human. He had issues fitting in, and Hugh had helped. But now Hugh had lost his own humanity somewhere along the line, and he needed Briggs to guide him back. He had been alienating to his sister, and now he had... He had come peril-ously close to besmirching his ward. To dishonouring his fiancée.

After his conversation with Briggs, he was satisfied that at least he had mended that first association. As for the rest... It would simply have to not happen again. There would be another ball. And another, and another. And he would see Eleanor married off. It was all that could be done.

It was what must be done.

'Your Grace.' The Madame in scarlet greeted him with a gentle curve of her lips.

Scarlet.

Red.

Claret.

Eleanor.

'I am sorry, Madame. I just realised I have somewhere else to be.'

Chapter Twelve

That night she wore lavender. And he couldn't take his eyes off her, no matter how hard he tried. Not that he tried all that hard. In fact, he'd contrived to place himself in an advantageous position in the ballroom, so that it wouldn't look as if he was following her every move.

And if ever Anna noticed, he simply commented that he was invested in Eleanor's acquisition of a husband. He might have tried to feed himself the same lie, but he was past that now.

He could no longer tell himself he cared only for her reputation, her marriage, her fate.

He wanted her.

And there was some perverse enjoyment he got out of taunting himself with her. Not only that night, but every night.

The next night was peach. And she was resplendent in that as well. Followed by buttercup. Mint. Periwinkle.

She cycled through each gown, each night, a confectionery treat, tempting him. Each colour emblazoned in his mind as if his words to the modiste were haunting him.

Was there anything more important on this whole earth than the colour of Eleanor's gowns? He was no longer certain.

Her beauty nearly destroyed him. Teasing him. By night, she was this angel, floating around before him, completely untouchable. And by day… By design he did not see her. They never encountered each other in the town house. As if they were both working to ensure that they never even passed one another in the corridors.

They took their meals at separate times, in separate spaces. He always ate in his chamber, or in his study.

He assumed she did the same.

Or perhaps she sat in that big dining room, all by herself.

It mattered not to him.

But the image of Eleanor, sitting there alone made him ache inside and he could not fathom why.

'And is Eleanor making any progress in her husband hunt?'

He looked away from Eleanor, back to Anna. Eleanor was in gold tonight. It was the first moment he had noticed what colour Anna was wearing. A dark blue. Sedate and perfect for the woman he meant to marry.

She did not shine like the stars.

Eleanor was the stars.

He swallowed past that thought. It was almost fantastical, and he was not a man who dealt in the fantastical.

'She does not seem any closer to making a decision,' he said, watching as Eleanor changed partners yet again.

'And when she has?'

'I will support her. Pay her dowry, as I promised her father I would, and be rid of her.' That, at least, was the truth. She might make him a liar when it came to the innermost parts of him. His desires. His needs. But she would not make him a liar in deed.

'You will be rid of her?' Anna asked, her eyebrows rising upward.

He frowned, uncertain of where her disbelief was coming from. 'Yes.'

Anna looked…vexed then, and he could not figure out why.

'I had thought you might be honest with me, at least,' she said.

'I do not understand.'

She let out a short, exasperated breath. 'Is she not your mistress, Hugh?'

Her words hit him with the force of a blow. And he was…shamed. Because no, Eleanor was not his mistress, but he wanted her. He was outraged by the suggestion, and yet, did he even have the right to be? When he wanted Eleanor, and only Eleanor, no matter that he played the perfect guardian for all the world? And did he? If Anna could see through to the heart of him, how convincing was he?

'How dare you suggest such a thing?' he asked, anger a rolling boil in his gut.

Her eyes widened. 'I am sorry if I have the wrong of it. You are distinctly uninterested in engaging me in a physical relationship, and you seem incapable of taking your eyes off her every time she's in the same room.'

'She's like a sister to me,' Hugh said, the lie tasting of metal on his tongue. 'With a reputation in a far more precarious position than a woman with a title ever could be. She is the daughter of a merchant. I promised her father I would see her wed. I promised her father I would protect her. One word of impropriety such as this and it would be the end of her.'

And that was not a lie.

If his desire put Eleanor at risk…

It did not bear thinking about.

'I'm sorry,' Anna said, looking away.

And he felt like the lowest of creatures, because he actually had touched Eleanor. He did want Eleanor. Anna wasn't spinning fables from the air. And he was happy to have her believe that she was.

He was the villain in this play. No question. None at all.

'So, you really are just that good?' she asked.

Those words lanced him, so unequal was he to such a statement. He was beginning to wonder if any good thing existed inside of him.

Or if he had simply never been adequately tested.

If all his life he had told himself he was better

than his father, only to discover now that he was no better at all.

He just had one, very different, very specific Achilles' heel.

Marry her off and it will no longer be an issue.

'I would never go so far as to say that,' he said.

And he did his best to not allow his eyes to land on Eleanor even one more time for the rest of the evening.

It had been a whirlwind of parties and balls for a week now. Not even one night off. And Eleanor couldn't say that she had any idea which of these men would propose to her. If any. She was starting to wonder if she was being thoroughly auditioned for the potential part of mistress.

Halfway through the Season and no one had made an offer for her.

Flowers were sent to the town house, and her dance card was full at every single event. But she was no closer to getting what she wanted. While Hugh had secured exactly what he wanted.

But she knew. And the secret burned between them. She could feel his eyes on her every night. She could feel it.

Damn the man.

She wanted him. And she knew that it would be the end of her.

And so she danced with Jared, the Earl of Gray-stone, who was a perfectly pleasant man, and who she had been meant to meet with in the garden the night she had kissed Hugh.

They hadn't had a chance to speak alone… Really ever. For they were always meant to be chaperoned. It was a strange thing, she thought, and not for the first time. 'Would you like to come out to the balcony with me? Just outside,' he said. 'Not to the garden.'

'I didn't…'

'You were quite right not to meet me. It was un-towards of me to make such an invitation.'

'I accepted it. I should have been brave enough to follow through.'

'You were wise not to. Come.'

He extended his arm and led her outside. It was a beautiful evening, the stars above twinkling, and she tried not to think of how she had compared her desire for Hugh to those stars. But she had a terrible feeling that she would be thinking of him for ever when she looked at the sky.

That she would think of *him* for ever.

'I think that it is quite obvious I have a great deal of affection for you,' the Earl said.

She thought about that for a moment. Affection? How did anyone come to believe they had affection for one another at these sorts of balls? Perhaps if he had come to call at the town house or visit her even just a few times… But he had not. They danced to-gether. He thought she was beautiful. She thought him blandly handsome.

She should be excited. He was on the verge of a

declaration, quite possibly. She should be excited, and she was not.

'I admire you a great deal,' she said.

'I am aware that there are many men here that are vying for your hand. But I should… I should like to speak to your guardian about making my intentions clear. I would like to ask him for your hand.'

'I see.'

'You do not seem pleased,' he said.

'I am. I am very pleased.' Why could she not manage to sound convincing? Even for a moment?

He was young. Younger than Hugh. A good-looking man. Titled. So far beyond that which she could ever have reached for otherwise. He was asking for her hand in marriage. He was not dishonouring her by making an offer for her to be his mistress. This was more than she could have ever hoped for.

'My dowry is quite generous,' she said.

Why had she said that? That was not what a lady would have done. Marriage was a business. It would keep her safe, and it would keep him rich. That was how it worked and she had no business embarrassing him by pointing that out.

Perhaps it mattered to him, perhaps it didn't.

But you want to know...

Because she was a foolish girl who wanted a man she gave nothing to.

Being with her would offer Hugh nothing.

He was a duke. Being with her would be lowering for him. Her money was his. She would offer him nothing except for herself.

And is that why you persist in wanting him so?

Maybe. It made her unbearably angry with herself. What was the point? Few women could aspire to such a thing. She was no one.

Why did she long for something so far out of her reach?

She watched Graystone's face while he considered what she'd said.

He nodded. 'Yes.' He watched her face to see if he'd hurt her. And she supposed she should care that he seemed to feel something for her.

That it mattered to him if she was bothered.

But she knew then that it was part of the enticement. She wondered what his debts were.

Then decided they didn't matter. Hugh's money would obliterate them. And she didn't have to marry an old man without teeth.

This was her moment. She should be utterly and totally relieved by it. ·

A handsome, strong, young man who would give her a life, security, children.

She should scream with joy over it. She should leap over the balcony and dance in the grass—though she would never do that because that would certainly damage her reputation.

But she just…couldn't.

She did not feel joy.

She did not feel relief.

She tried to imagine kissing the Earl of Graystone as she had kissed Hugh. She could not imagine it. Not now. But maybe it would never come to that.

Perhaps passion would never explode between them.

He would spend her money, and she would give him an heir. And she would be protected. That should be a dream. It should be a fantasy.

A beautiful one, in this world of broken, distorted things where society had the power to choose so much of what they were.

And within the realm of possible things, it was a very, very good outcome.

But she wanted the impossible.

She wanted the stars.

'I shall come by tomorrow to speak to him.'

'Yes,' she said, nodding, her throat dry. 'That is very good.'

And if he seemed to sense her hesitance, he did not speak about it. Instead, he took her hand, lowered his head and kissed her knuckles. 'We will be a good match.'

'We will be a good match,' she repeated.

Because it was true. They would be the sort of match that people would rave about. Good for them both. She marrying above her station, and he coming into money.

'Shall we join the party? I will not do anything to bring scandal upon your name.'

'Thank you,' she said. And the whole thing was as bland and wonderful as he was. She realised now that perhaps it had been a test. Perhaps if she had gone out to the garden with him she would've merely been his mistress. No. He needed the money, so she could have been a wife, fallen or not. But he was now treating her with great respect because he thought her a woman of virtue. What would he think if he knew? If he knew that she had been in Hugh's arms when she had promised to be in his?

When they went back into the ballroom, her eyes caught Hugh's immediately. And somehow, she could tell that he knew.

Chapter Thirteen

The boy was in his study. And he was a boy, as far as Hugh was concerned.

'I should like to ask for your permission to wed Miss Jennings.'

'I see,' he said. 'And does Miss Jennings return your affections?'

The boy had not spoken of affections. Hugh asked about them all the same. If he had not caught Eleanor in the garden, it was this boy whose arms she would have found herself in. Did she want that? Even as she wanted him?

Had she told him the truth that night in his study? Was it not him she wanted, but a taste of passion itself?

'Such as they are,' he said slowly. 'She seems to like me a great deal.'

'Well. Many marriages have been built on less than that.'

It was true. Hugh should respect the boy for not declaring his undying love for a woman he'd scarcely courted. He wanted her dowry, and there was nothing amiss about that. He had treated her with propriety and he was now offering for her hand.

There was no reason for Hugh to deny him.

It was raining. And that felt suitable. It had been perfectly clear in London these past few nights, and now it was a torrential downpour outside. When the Earl had arrived, he'd seen Eleanor, peering from the top of the stairs. Clearly, she knew why he was here as well as Hugh did.

'Tell me about yourself,' he said, though he found he did not care to hear his answers. 'About your circumstances.'

'We have a small estate in London. And also a larger one in the country. I would be remiss if I were not honest about the fact that there are… Debts.'

Hugh froze, a muscle in his face twitching. 'Of which variety?'

'Gambling.' The other man fought to keep Hugh's gaze even as he admitted this and Hugh found himself reluctantly respecting him for that. Elevating him from boy to man in his thoughts. 'Though… It ensnared my father, and I found myself going down the same path. Mostly because at first I wanted to fix it. I wanted to gain back what he had lost. And now I realise that isn't going to happen. I realise that I must be more circumspect. With this dowry I will be able to put things to rights. And I swear I will not squander any of it.'

'A very bold promise,' he said.

'I did not wish to lie to you,' he said, and had it

been another moment, Hugh might've admired the honesty. But as it was he could admire nothing about this man. This man who was asking for Eleanor's hand. Who seemed unequal to her and yet...

Hugh had no real reason to deny him. He was exactly the sort of man she ought to be with.

He sat at the desk and looked outside at the garden behind the town house. And he saw movement. Just a bit.

And then she came into his full view, her golden hair soaking wet, and the pale pink gown she wore sticking to her skin. She was looking up at the rain, the water droplets rolling down her face.

She was too great a temptation to bear.

She was too beautiful to bear. He could not be expected to stand against such a thing. And here he had his chance. This moment. To give her away. To be rid of her as he had promised Anna that he would be. To make what he had said to her the truth. That he had only honourable designs, that he would see her married off and be done with her.

He had this moment. He had his chance.

But he could only look at her. It was all he could ever do.

'I'm sorry to disappoint you,' he said. 'I am. But she does not speak of you. And your debts don't speak well of you.'

'Your Grace...' Colour mounted in the younger man's cheeks, and Hugh had no doubt that if he were not the Duke of Kendal, the man would have raised his fist to him. But as it was, he would not. As it was, he would do nothing but sit there, gulping like a fish drowning in the air.

'You will have to find another person to redeem you. It is not Miss Jennings's job to do so.'

Colour mounted in the Earl's face. 'Your Grace, with all due respect, she is a merchant's daughter.' And even now he was not being spiteful. He simply spoke the truth.

But it made Hugh's blood burn.

'I am aware of her origins. After all, it is how she came to be in my care, however, she is in my care. And it is up to me to decide what is best for her. It is not up to you, and it is not up to anyone else. You are not what is best for her.'

Liar.

He seemed to take the full measure of Hugh for a moment before nodding once, in a curt fashion. 'Your Grace.'

Then he turned on his heel, leaving like a coward. Leaving like a man who had no real feelings for her, for if he was beset by passion he would have argued. But instead he left. With his tail between his legs, and Hugh could *not* respect that.

He looked out of the window, at the sodden grey.

There was Eleanor, out in the garden, with the rain cascading over her, and he knew that she expected to hear that she was an engaged woman. He was about to disappoint her.

He waited until the Earl had left the house, until he heard the front door open and close and the servant see him off. And then he went down the stairs, out through the back door into the garden.

Her back faced away from him, her shoulders shaking.

'You'll catch your death,' he said.

The rain was leaving spots on his grey morning coat. It seemed significant.

She turned. 'I assume you're here to tell me the happy news.'

'If the happy news is that you will not be marrying the Earl of Graystone.'

'I… I won't?'

'I denied him.'

'You… You denied him?'

'Yes. You do not need to ask for clarification when I have spoken so succinctly on the subject. You are not confused, Eleanor, and we both know it.'

'But I am. He is far beyond anything that I ever… He is above me in every way, Your Grace. And you do not have the right to deny me what I want so very badly.'

'You do not want him.'

She gasped, her shoulders lifting sharply. 'I do not want him? *I do not want him?* How dare you? How dare you play games with my fate like this. Do you know what I want? What I want is to be free of this. To be free of *you.* What I want is to have successfully… I want to be finished, Hugh. I don't want to fight any more. I'm tired of waiting to find out if I will survive this game. Will I find a husband, or will I be doomed to live life as some man's mistress? I found a man who wished to marry me.' The words were raw, torn from her, and he felt a moment of regret, and yet it was not strong enough to make him change course.

'He has gambling debts.'

'I suspected as much,' she said. 'I knew that what he wanted was my money.'

'My money,' Hugh said. 'And I do not find him worthy of it. Or of you.'

'I'm not going to marry a duke, Hugh. I'm not Beatrice. I'm not going to get a man who doesn't need to gain something from marriage to me. Otherwise why would he simply not put me up in a house somewhere in town and call upon me when it suits him? Why would a man make me his wife unless he needed the dowry?' Her eyes were round and bleak, and he hated it. 'I am nothing on my own, Hugh. Nothing.'

He gritted his teeth, her words tearing through him like a wild beast. She was not nothing. How could she say that?

He stood in the rain for her, she was not nothing.

He had kissed her while engaged to another, she was not nothing.

She was turning him into a man he did not recognise.

She was not nothing.

'I do not approve of gambling debts,' he said. 'There are many other innocuous reasons why a man might need…'

'Enough. Call him back. Fix this. You cannot consign me to this fate. It isn't fair. You have secured your engagement, and you insist on denying me mine.'

'I do not insist on denying you anything. It is only that you must be rational. You must be reasonable.'

'Like you? Like you always are.'

Anger flared through him. And he found himself closing the distance between them. A single sheet of rain fell in the space left betwixt their bodies. 'He is not good enough for you.'

'It matters not what you think. When they all know that I am not good enough for any of them. You are a pompous ass. I'm tired of you playing with me.'

And she looked at him, her beautiful face up-turned, the water rolling down her cheeks.

And he could resist no longer. He wrapped his arms around her and pulled her up against him. Leaving not even enough space for a single raindrop to fit between them.

And he kissed her again.

Chapter Fourteen

Bitter hopelessness poured through her, even as the rain poured down onto her. She had come out here to grieve. To let go of her fantasies while Hugh secured her future during his discussion with the Earl of Graystone. And then, he had done the unthinkable. He had denied her. And it could not be borne. Not when he was taking so much from her. And then he kissed her. Kissed her as if they were not impossible. Kissed her as if he had a right to her.

And she realised she wasn't even strong enough to resist.

She melted into him. Parted her lips for him. Gave herself over to him as she had done in the garden. She was desperate now. Shivering from the cold, from her distress, and he moved his hands over her body, moved to cup her cheek, wiping raindrops from her skin. And then he licked her, lapping at the water droplets on her lips.

He wrapped his hand around the sleeve of her dress and pulled it down, revealing one breast to the freezing air. Her nipple went tight, and she knew that she should be horrified. Embarrassed. Then his strong, hot hand closed over her flesh, and she could only whimper with desire. Shiver with her need for him. And he continued to kiss her. To devour her. As if there was nothing else but this. Nothing else but them.

He lowered his head then, taking her nipple deep into his mouth, sucking hard.

She gasped, arching against him, and he rubbed his face against her skin. The rasp from his whiskers sent an arrow of desire down between her legs. 'I'm sorry,' he said, his voice rough.

Then he picked her up off the ground, pulled her dress back into place, and carried her into the house.

He did not break stride when they went inside. He carried her up the stairs, putting more stock in the propriety of household staff than she ever would.

And she was carried straight to his bedchamber. He brought her inside and set her down, closing the door firmly behind them. 'I am sorry,' he said, meeting her gaze and grabbing hold of her chin with his thumb and forefinger. 'But I need you. Do you need me?'

And she realised that she would give it all to him. All of it. He was engaged to another woman, and he could not ever wed her. Never. And she would be his mistress. She would live in the shadows. In the margins. Become the sort of woman that even her dear friend Beatrice could no longer speak to because he would not allow his sister to associate with his paramour.

She had been taught to avoid this all her life. But right now, she knew it had been her fate from the moment she had first walked into his home.

For there was not another man. There couldn't be. She would live in shadow. And she would have his bastards. And she would have just a piece of him. And he would go home to his real house every night, to his real children. To his real wife. And she would take it. And she wanted to weep. Not with sadness, but with the relief that she was finally allowing herself to admit that she would take him that way. If all she could have was a piece, then she would take that piece. And it would be beautiful. Better than a loveless marriage with a man she didn't want.

You are a foolish girl.

She heard it in Missy's voice.

But what did she know? She had been a mistress, and it had been for love. And maybe her father had no longer been married, but she'd lived in the margins all the same. She'd had no security when he died. She'd had nothing.

But she had been with a man that she loved.

And Eleanor was willing in that moment to make the trade. To make the sacrifice. She was willing.

No, it was something more than willing. It was need.

She wanted to be wanted. She wanted to be everything.

She offered Hugh Ashforth, the Duke of Kendal, nothing. Except for her heart. Except for her body. Except for her soul.

And he wanted it.

Wanted her.

It was more than she could have ever had with the Earl, even while it was astonishingly less. She doubted most would understand.

She wasn't certain she understood.

But it felt right.

For the first time in so long, something felt right.

She had spent years denying the depth of her feeling, her longing, and here and now she could let it all come to the surface. She could act as she felt, not act as a being who had to perform independently of who she was in her heart.

That had to count for something.

It had to.

'Yes,' she said. And she said it with more conviction that she had been able to muster up for the Earl's proposal. 'Yes,' she said again, kissing his mouth, wrapping her arms around his neck and touching him. Finally touching him, knowing that it wouldn't end.

She wasn't afraid. Yes. She would be ruined. But it was by her choice. She would be ruined, and she would have chosen it.

And there was no shame. Not in her. People would want her to feel shame. They would be ashamed of her.

But she didn't care. Beatrice would understand. They would continue their friendship, even if it had to be in secret. But she would understand, because she was willing to risk her very life to have a baby with the man that she loved. Eleanor wasn't risking her life. Just her position in society, which had only ever been tenuous at best. Which had only ever been connected to him.

So the fact that he would be her downfall was quite all right. It truly was.

She kissed him on a sob, and he began to tear at her gown. Peeling the cold, wet fabric away from her skin with ruthless efficiency.

She tugged at his cravat, pushed his coat away from his shoulders.

And gasped the moment his shirt parted, revealing the muscular chest that she had so longed to touch. She slipped her hand beneath the wet fabric and shuddered.

He grabbed hold of her hand and brought her fingertips to his mouth, biting the edge of one, and she felt an erotic tug between her legs.

'I do not know how to be with a virgin,' he said. 'I can only warn you.'

She moved nearer to him, put her face against the crook of his neck. She whispered, her lips against his skin. 'Don't be with a virgin. Be with me.'

'A lovely sentiment, but it doesn't mean you are not an innocent.'

'Nothing that I feel for you is innocent,' she said. 'I lie awake at night and I think of you. Of your hands. Of your mouth.'

He took her hand and brought it down to the front of his breeches, ran it over the hard, masculine part of his body that made her eyes widen.

'If you have not thought of this, then you are an innocent. And it does in fact matter.'

She felt nothing but a thrill. Wasn't this what Missy had told her? That a man would want to impale her with that part of him. And by that instrument she would be ruined. It can be pleasurable. It can also be painful. At the very least that first time will be.

She wasn't afraid of that. She found that she was quite unafraid of everything. There was something glorious in surrender on this level. And knowing that she was becoming the thing that she had feared the most. But that she was choosing it.

'I'm not afraid,' she said. 'I want you inside of me.'

He growled then, gripping her chin tight and dragging her to him for a bruising kiss that left her weak. He finished stripping every article of clothing from her body, leaving her pale and shivering, wet. He stood back and looked at her. 'You're glorious. More than I even imagined.'

'Did you imagine?' Her voice sounded thin and breathless, and needy. And she might have despised that if she had not made this devil's bargain. Why should he not know how much she wanted him? Shouldn't he know, considering all she was trading?

'When you made me that cake. Then... I was consumed with you. What girl thinks of such a thing? It was such a simple thing. And it got you in my head. Under my skin. I cannot stop... I thought of pulling your dress down so that I could see your body. I thought of licking you. Sucking you. Tasting between your legs.'

She shivered. His words were erotic, and so un-like the man that she knew. And yet... The intensity was there. The intensity that was all Hugh. And always would be.

'There's nothing to stop you.'

He growled. And he began to strip off his clothing, revealing that masculine torso, those well-defined muscles.

His hands went to the falls of his breeches, and she watched as he unveiled himself. He made quick work of his boots although they were fitted tight to him. And soon he was naked, glorious in front of her. She had never seen a naked man. Never anything more than a rather limp looking statue. And he was nothing like that. He wasn't cold marble. And he did not simply hang loosely between his thighs. No. He stood out, thick and proud from his body. His chest was broad, sprinkled with golden hair, his stomach tight and rippling. His thighs strong and well-muscled from riding.

Her mouth watered.

She craved this man. Perhaps this was it. Perhaps it was blood telling on her. Her, and blood. For she was just a woman willing to dive headfirst into iniquity, as long as he was there.

A lady would not. A lady would be shocked by this, her first sight of a naked aroused male. But she was not a lady.

And she never had been.

She was a merchant's daughter, and today she did not fall from grace.

She jumped from it.

She moved towards him, put her hand on his chest. 'Hugh,' she said. And he did not ask her to call him Your Grace. No. He was Hugh. And she was Eleanor. And that was how they would be when they were together like this. It was who they would be to each other from now on. He crushed her bare body against his, bringing his mouth down to hers in a hard kiss. His teeth pressed against her bottom lip, and she was certain that she tasted blood.

It was a frenzy. A fury. He seemed overcome by passion, and she was swept up in the tide. He lowered his head to her breasts, and with his large hands, he pressed them together, moving his tongue quickly across both her nipples, ratcheting her pleasure up, higher and higher. There was no embarrassment. No shame. She was going to be his mistress. The mistress of the Duke. The woman in the shadows.

The woman who had his passion.

And she would give as good as she got. He picked her up then, and laid her down on his bed, looming over her, his sharp gaze almost as intense as physical touch.

Like a wanton, she arched her back, and on some instinct, parted her thighs. He growled, coming down over the top of her, his hands bruising on her hips, his male member like an iron rod against that soft, damp place between her legs.

'Temptress,' he said.

'Is that what I am?'

'I have lived above reproach,' he said, his forehead

pressed against hers. 'For all these years. I have done everything that was expected of me. And you were the one thing that I could not come to grips with. You, this young chit of a girl I should have had no trouble resisting. And how do you like that? You've made me what I swore never to become. You have made me into my father.'

'Maybe I haven't,' she said. 'Maybe you just never knew what it was to want something so much that you were willing to abandon your principles for it.'

'I do want you.' The words were broken. 'I want to plunge into your tight body. I want to leave bruises on your skin, does that shock you?'

And this man, she didn't know. She had always known Hugh, the upstanding Duke of Kendal, who had indeed been above reproach. She had never known this man. Rough and dangerous, making filthy promises that made her feel electrified.

And she didn't fear being marked by him. For if she could not have vows in public declarations, then she would take those declarations on her skin.

She was afraid of nothing. Not from him.

She would be his. In whatever manner he demanded.

'Yes,' she said. 'Make me yours.'

He growled, and turned her over onto her stomach, running his hand down her spine, to her buttocks. He squeezed her, then lifted his hand and brought it down with a firm crack. Pain glanced her, along with pleasure, which bloomed insistently and greedily between her legs.

He kissed a path down her spine, to where he had just struck her. He bit her there. Kissed her. Then moved down further to the damp crease between her legs, flicking his tongue over her. He spread her open for him in that prone position, and tasted her, until she was squirming. Until she was crying out for more. He speared her with a finger, working it in and out of her tight channel. And she wiggled against him, silently begging for more. He added another finger, and it burned.

But she ached for him. For more of him. 'Please,' she begged. 'Please.'

He turned her onto her back again, cupped her breasts for a moment, flicking his thumbs over her nipples before settling himself between her legs, rubbing that hardened rod between her slick folds until she was panting with desire. Then he leaned down and kissed her there, suckling that sensitised bundle of nerves between his lips. She shattered. Utterly and completely. And while she was sobbing out her pleasure, he positioned himself between her legs again, the blunt head of his arousal testing the slick entrance to her body. And then he thrust home. It hurt. But only for a moment. And after that blinding pain ended, there was nothing but pleasure. Connection. She could not tell where he ended and she began. It was as if they were one and the same.

And for all her life she knew she could never regret this. To be ruined by the man she loved was a gift. Even as it was a curse.

And as he thrust into her, over and over again, she

said his name like a prayer. His first name. For she did not call him Your Grace. And even Anna would likely always refer to him by his title. But not Eleanor. Not Eleanor. And when a second wave of pleasure broke over her, it coincided with his.

And as he roared out his release, she clung to his shoulders and whispered in his ear. 'Hugh.'

At the same time he said, 'I'm sorry.'

Chapter Fifteen

It was dark in the bedchamber. Because the curtains were closed. She could see him, though.

Next to her in bed.

He was on top of the bedclothes, on his stomach.

It was the strangest thing. To be in bed with Hugh. He was naked, and she could look at him. Touch him. So she did. She ran her fingers down the centre of his back, down further still, and she marvelled as his body began to stir.

'You're beautiful,' she whispered.

He was dozing, and in all the years she'd known him she had never seen him sleep. She had never seen him naked. She had never been alone with him quite like this. And this was why. It all made sense now. Now that she had jumped into a life of ruination. She could understand it all. This was why women had to be so careful.

Because passion was overwhelming. And the consequences all seemed… Reasonable. When he had touched her, it had all seemed reasonable. And she realised that what she had determined only a couple of hours ago was folly. For many reasons. The biggest of which was…

She could not be with him like this when he had a wife.

The thought made her physically ill.

How had she thought she might share him?

And Anna would *know*. Every night she wasn't in bed with him, she would know. Just as Eleanor would know where he was when he wasn't in bed with her.

And it had all seemed bearable when it had been a choice between that and never touching him again. It all seemed bearable then.

And even now she didn't regret her ruination. She had no choice now, though. She could escape still without rumour attached to her. But she was a fallen woman, there was no denying it. No escaping it. She would go to Beatrice, who would help her. She would understand. She would understand why Eleanor had made this choice, and Briggs would write her reference. She was certain of that. She would be able to find a position as a governess.

She didn't have to be a mistress.

And you'll be alone. For ever. For the rest of your life.

She wouldn't be alone. She could salvage her reputation, and she could have her friend.

She couldn't have Hugh either way. That was the thing. Not really.

She lay there another moment. Looking at him.

And she thought of all those beautiful dresses in her room that she wouldn't get to wear. And nearly laughed, because she would've traded them all in for a few hours of wearing nothing with him. And she had. She knew things about herself now. She knew things about mistresses she hadn't known before. And that was the real problem.

It was the knowing. Knowing that sharing him meant he would be inside another woman, lying next to her. That she would watch him sleep. It was these little things that in her innocence she had not fully understood. That she did now.

Yes. It was those things she could not overlook.

She leaned in and kissed him, just at the corner of his mouth. She was so weak. Part of her would have debased herself for the chance to have this for ever.

She'd jumped high enough to be among the stars, just for a moment. But she'd fallen back to earth now.

How could she have children with him and expose them to a life of scorn?

How could she...

She hated Anna. In this moment, she hated her, and yet. She could not do that to the other woman, any more than she could do it to herself.

She looked at him, his broad shoulders, the muscles of his back, that gloriously male behind, his thighs. And she committed him to memory. Every inch. He would be her only lover. The thought made her indescribably sad. Not because she wanted to be with other men. But because now she knew the beauty of it. And she wanted it with him. For ever. But all she would have was this memory.

She held back tears as she gathered her clothes. Her dress was wet. But she got herself together as best she could before going to her bedroom and putting on a simple blue dress. Then she packed an overnight bag. And walked down the stairs, carefully timing her steps to avoid the household staff. It was not a long walk to the town house where Briggs and Beatrice were. And it would be better if the staff weren't certain of where she had gone.

No one was there to attend her, and she slipped out through the front door without notice. The staff knew. She was sure of that. She hoped it would not come back on her. She truly did hope so. Her chest felt like it was filled with stones, and by the time she arrived at Beatrice's house, she was near tears. But she held it together all the way until she was admitted into her friend's sitting room. And then she pressed her hand over her mouth to stifle a sob.

'Oh, no,' Beatrice said. 'What has my brother done?'

She was gone. She was not in bed when he woke up, and no one on his staff had any clue where she'd run off to.

He could only hope that she was not in distress. She had wanted… He was certain of it. He was certain that what had happened between them was mutual. That it was something she wanted as much as he did.

Wherever she was, it didn't matter. There was something he had to do.

He left the town house, walking to Anna's home.

'Good afternoon, Lady Paxton,' he said.

She looked at him with concern in her eyes. And the concern was warranted.

'To what do I owe the pleasure, Your Grace?'

But she was a smart woman, and he could see that she knew already.

'I'm here to pass along my greatest regret. I cannot marry you.'

'Your Grace…'

'You will be fine. It will be my disgrace, and not yours. This is the second engagement that has ended for me, and it will be clear to all those who witnessed…'

For the first time since he'd met her, she looked afraid. 'No, Your Grace. I think you do not understand. I think you don't understand what it means to be a woman. And why should you? It does not matter if this is your second broken engagement, it will be me who faces scorn. To have been put away by you so shortly after you grandly announce our engagement.'

Pain lanced him. For he was doing exactly what he had sworn he would not. He was his father. In every way. He had ruined Eleanor, and he had to make amends for that. It was why he had apologised to her, even as he had taken her into his arms. Because he had known then that there was no going back. That he would have her. And that she would have to become his wife. And whatever she thought, it would not be a kindness for her. She was not the sort of woman who was built to be the Duchess of Kendal. Their association, and the origins of it would taint everything. His broken engagements…

None of it was a favour to any of the women involved, and he knew that. It was why he had apologised. And she might be hiding out at the moment, but she wouldn't stay gone. They had to marry. She could even be with child now.

'I will ensure that it does not reflect poorly on you. And as time marches on, believe me when I tell you it will all become apparent. And no one will have a bad thing to say about you.'

'You misunderstand the society that you are a part of, Your Grace. And how can you not? You occupy nearly the highest rung in it. You stand next to the king. Of course you do. You are a man above reproach.'

'I am not. I hold myself to greater accountability than that, and I do not allow myself to be forgiven at all just now. I do not. I have used you badly, and I did not intend to.'

'At least tell me…'

'Eleanor is not my…mistress. She was my ward all these years and that is the truth. I was not carrying on a relationship with her while planning to marry you.' He chose his next words carefully, for he felt he owed Anna honesty, but he also wished to protect Eleanor as much as he could. 'Now, however, I do need to make her my wife.'

She went pale. 'I see.'

'It is a matter of honour.'

'And you give me this information as if I will not use it against you. Against her.'

'I am giving you honesty. However foolish it might be. Though I trust that you are every bit the woman that I thought you were when I asked you to be my wife. I truly did believe... I do believe...that you would be best suited to the position of Duchess of Kendal, of any woman that I could have chosen.'

Anna nodded slowly, her expression serene now. 'It is only that you have not selected with your brain.'

He deserved that.

'No,' he said. 'I have not.'

'I wish you the best of luck, Your Grace.'

'And you as well. I will not allow a bad word to be spoken of you...'

'But I'm not yours, Your Grace. And my life is my own. You have chosen to protect another. And you must do so. Because if you have ruined her, then we both know what you must do.' She smiled vaguely. 'I thank you now for your restraint with me.'

That landed like a closed fist, and it should have. He deserved it. 'I truly never intended to harm you.'

'The worst part is I believe you. I believe you, and I cannot even hate you. Though I should like to. Very much.'

With that deed done, he walked out of the town house. Recrimination would come, even if it didn't come directly from Anna herself.

It would come soon enough.

When he got back to the town house, Eleanor still wasn't there.

He went into his study. And he waited.

'I just need a reference,' she said.

'Eleanor, of course we will give you whatever you wish...'

'I was a fool, Beatrice. I thought that I could be his mistress. I thought that I would be all right. But I can't. I can't.'

'Of course not,' Beatrice said. 'It's unbearable. I would never be able to share Briggs with another woman. Least of all if he was married to another. And my brother owes you so much more than that.'

She shook her head. 'Beatrice. You know the way of the world. Your brother owes me nothing. And I was warned. I was duly warned about this kind of thing. My father's mistress... She told me how it was for women. Women like me. She told me I had to be above reproach, and the moment... The moment that I had temptation set before me I failed.'

'To be absolutely fair to you, it has been a long-held desire. You did not crumble at the drop of a hat. You crumbled beneath the weight of years of wanting. I understand that well. Even though I didn't realise quite how I felt about Briggs...'

'I understand.' She sighed. 'As long as I can escape with my reputation...and become a governess. But I need to be away from him. I cannot allow him to have this kind of hold over me any more. He's going to marry Anna Paxton and I...'

'He's a fool,' Beatrice said. 'You have mine and Briggs's full support.'

She realised then that no matter what, she would never be as alone as she'd feared. She would have Beatrice. She would have Briggs.

She had more than Missy had. She had real friends.

They were family, in a sense, and she hadn't fully ever realised that. That she had this.

She wanted to weep with her relief, with her broken heart. With everything.

'Thank you for not judging me.'

'Of course I don't judge you,' Beatrice said. 'I completely understand what it's like. How can I judge you knowing what an overwhelming force passion is. It truly changes everything.'

It had. It had changed her entire understanding of the world. Her understanding of herself. It had changed absolutely everything. And she could never go back to seeing things the way she had done before. She could never go back.

'And what shall I do in the meantime?'

'You'll stay with us. Of course you will. You're family, Eleanor. And I don't care if you were made to feel like anything less, it isn't true. You're family to me. The closest thing to a sister I've ever had. I will always see you as my sister.'

She loved that image. But she knew it wasn't true. It couldn't be. Because she could never be here when Hugh came to call with his wife in tow. She couldn't stand seeing his children.

The thought of children made her pale.

'I could be with child,' she said.

'Very likely not,' Beatrice said. 'I'm still not, and not for Briggs's lack of effort. It often takes time.'

'I can only hope that the time required was not taken.'

'We will outfit you a room.'

'Thank you. And if he… If he comes looking for me…'

'I will refuse to tell him where you are. But I will tell him that you're safe.'

'And you don't think he's going to shout at you until you tell him exactly which room I'm staying in?'

'I'm not afraid of my brother. I had to get away from him to make my own life. That you must do the same is something I understand.'

She still wasn't home. Where the hell was she?

Without thinking, he got on his horse and rode directly to Briggs and Beatrice's town house. It was his friend who answered the door, as if he was a common merchant, his shirt and cuffs undone, a glass of whisky in his hand. 'Good evening,' he said. 'You are interrupting.'

Anger burned through him. 'Just because I accept that the nature of your relationship with my sister has changed, and just because I am no longer actively opposed to it does not mean I need to know when you are…' he felt his lip curl, 'at play.'

'Then don't show up unannounced. If you come during playtime…'

'You did not have to answer the door.'

Briggs looked him over. 'I think I did. Do I need to ask why you're here?'

'Where is Eleanor?'

His sister appeared then, her hair half down. 'That is none of your business.'

'For God's sake,' he said, taking in her dishevelled appearance.

'God has nothing to do with it,' Briggs said. 'Though she does sometimes call me that.'

'Where is she?' he asked, his patience wearing decidedly thin.

'She is safe. But as to where she is, that is not your business, Hugh,' his sister said, her forcefulness a shock. 'How dare you? How dare you ruin her. And expect that she will simply live a half-life as your mistress...'

'Why would you think that?' he asked.

'I saw her this afternoon. I saw the truth of it. You ruined her. And you are engaged to another woman... You sent away the man who wished to marry her. What other conclusion is there to draw?'

And for the first time in his life, something had eluded him completely. He had not even considered that Eleanor could believe that he... That he would have her in that way and not offer marriage. That he would marry another woman. Was his reputation truly worth nothing? Had he spent his entire life behaving as a man above reproach for no reason at all? Everyone thought the worst of him regardless of what he did. And yes, he had behaved with a certain reckless abandon.

'I will marry her,' he said.

'But you're engaged.'

'Not as of this afternoon. How could you think that of me?'

'You were going to prevent me from marrying, and then when I did marry, you thought that it was your business whether or not my marriage was consummated. I don't put very much past you.'

'What I did, I have done only for the protection of those around me. And what I did not do with Eleanor for years was for her own protection. I am a man who prizes control above all else. And my failure here is not something I take lightly. I am not our father.'

And even as he said it he feared that he was. He feared it to his bones.

'I can speak to her tomorrow,' Beatrice said.

'I wish to speak to her now. Tell me where she is.'

'I promised her that I would not,' Beatrice said.

'You are my sister.'

'And she is a woman. And I stand with her in solidarity of that. You are a duke, Hugh, and you will never understand what it is to be anything else.'

'You were the second woman to say that to me today.'

'Perhaps it would benefit you to begin listening.'

'And you?' he asked his friend.

'I know better than to defy my wife.'

'I've half a mind to tear apart your entire household.'

'My son is sleeping,' Briggs said. 'And if you wake him, I will be forced to kill you. Also, should you tear apart my house, I guarantee you will find things you wish you hadn't seen.'

'I will speak to her tomorrow.'

He was already turning and walking out of the town house.

He closed the door firmly behind him, and stood out on the front street, looking back up at the façade of the place. And there was one window with a flickering light, on the third floor, down at the end.

The servants would not be there. And if William was asleep, then there would be no light in his nursery. He was a duke. On that score Beatrice was correct. And that meant he did not have to take no for an answer.

He just had to forge a new path.

There was only one way forward. And he was not afraid to take that path. But he would need a carriage.

She was just finishing brushing her hair when she heard a loud thump at the window. She turned just in time to see it fly open, as Hugh, leading with his elbow, stepped into her room.

'Those locks are not very effective at all.'

'What are you doing in here?'

She clutched her hands to her chest, covering her nightdress as if he had not seen her completely nude just this afternoon.

As if she were a maiden with virtue left to protect.

'Eleanor…' His voice was shattered. Ragged.

'What are you…'

And then he walked forward, wrapped his arms around her waist, and threw her over his shoulder.

'Hugh!'

'You're coming with me.'

'What are you doing?'

And she found herself being hauled out through the third-floor window. Her heart slammed against her breastbone, and she clung to him in sheer terror as he used a combination of window ledges and vines to carry them both down to the ground.

'Are you insane?'

'We will find out.'

He opened the door to a sleek black carriage, and bodily put her inside, closing the door behind them both, her heart pounding wildly out of control.

'What are you doing?'

He took his open hand and rapped the top of the carriage, and it lurched forward, moving quickly, much faster than the usual pace.

'Where are we going?'

She could feel the carriage careening through the streets of London. This had to be dangerous.

'That is none of your concern.'

'But it is, Hugh. You cannot… You cannot force me to go back there. You cannot force me to be your mistress. I ran away because I decided that I… I cannot. And I won't.'

'My mistress?' He laughed. He *laughed*. 'You silly girl.'

'How am I a silly girl? I was silly to let you kiss

me. Silly to let you strip me of my virtue. That's what was silly. That's what…'

'Quiet. We are not going back to the town house. And you are not going to be my mistress. We are going to Gretna Green. You will be my wife by morning.'

Chapter Sixteen

She scrambled to the other side of the carriage. *Married?*

She hadn't realised that she'd asked that question out loud until he responded to it. 'Yes. We are to be married. With haste.'

'You are engaged.'

'I am not, as it happens. As of this afternoon. And if my ridiculous sister had bothered to let me speak to you earlier today, you would've known that, and we all could have been spared this bit of dramatics. But my hand was forced.'

'You could've waited. This didn't have to be done now. It doesn't have to be done now.'

'But you see,' he said. 'I have an affliction. It is called being a duke. And everyone that I've spoken to today has informed me that my being a duke makes it impossible for me to understand the plight of others. Makes it impossible for me to be invested in anything other than my own wants and needs. I have decided to embrace this. Which means, no, Eleanor, I cannot wait. We will be married at sunrise, the moment this carriage reaches Scotland.'

'This is going to create a scandal.'

'You are the scandal,' he said, his voice hard, uncompromising. 'You. If we announce our engagement here, wait for the banns to be read, if we take our time, it will still be a scandal. All the years we shared a house, travelled together...they will assume I ruined you.'

'You don't know...'

'And they are correct. The only thing that matters is we marry. As quickly as possible. It cannot wait another moment. I cannot wait. We will go to Gretna Green, and we will stay in Scotland as long as we need to. I have a family home there, though I have not visited in more than a decade.'

'You're going to marry me?' And for a moment she was dizzy. 'But you *are* engaged?'

'I'm not,' he said, his voice rough. 'I woke to discover you gone and the first thing I did was go and visit Anna. I told her that I must regretfully break things off between the two of us. Because the moment that I kissed you, you stupid girl, I knew that I would have to marry you. The moment that I carried you into that house. Do you think for one second that I would've debauched you in that way without making you mine? Such a low opinion that you have of me.'

'I...' And she began to cry. Fat drops of tears rolling down her cheeks. Her entire body beginning to shake. 'You're going to marry me?'

She wished she could stop crying, but she couldn't. Beatrice had hidden her away, pledged loyalty to her no matter what. But all the while he'd been intent on marrying her. He was going to marry her.

He was going to marry her and gain nothing. He would marry her just to spare her and it made her tears run hotter, faster.

'There is nothing else to be done,' he said.

He did not move to comfort her. He did not soften because of her tears.

'Why didn't you say so?' she asked, rubbing at her cheeks.

'Was it not apparent?'

'No.' She gave a watery laugh. 'No, you fool. It was not. I thought…'

'I would've thought it was clear that I would never dishonour you in such a fashion.'

'It isn't clear. Because we have been dancing around this truth for all these years. And there has barely been an honest word between us. It has been nothing more than barbs traded back and forth and barely leashed incivility. Why would I presume to know the rules to your game? And it is your game, Hugh, whether you want to hear that or not. You are the Duke, and I am not.'

'It is not a game. The moment I had you in my bed you had to be mine.'

'And what will people say?'

'Absolutely everything that I always feared they would say. It will rebound upon my mother. My sister, thank God, is married to a duke of her own, no matter how debauched he might be. She will be fine.'

'And me?'

'There is not going to be a way to hide the circumstances of this.'

'You making the decision for the two of us to run away to Gretna Green isn't going to make matters better.'

'It's either that or secure a special license, which obviously can be done, but I would rather this be handled by the time any potential seed takes root in your womb.'

'You fear I'm with child?'

'Yes. A valid fear. I took no precaution.'

'Precautions can be taken?'

He looked at her, his expression flat. 'Did you not know?'

'How would I know?'

'I thought your father's mistress spoke to you of the realities of life.'

'Yes. She did. But she didn't tell me a woman could avoid getting herself with child. Though I suppose she managed as my father's mistress all those years without ever bearing him a son.'

'It doesn't matter. I took no precaution with you. Because as I said, the decision was made.'

'You said you were sorry.'

He paused for a long moment. 'And I am.'

'I assumed you meant because you were condemning me to a life as your mistress.'

'I am condemning you to life as my wife. And believe me when I tell you, that is not especially something to rejoice about.'

And she realised then that she would know him now in an entirely new way. His wife. Hugh's wife. Hugh had broken into her bedroom and kidnapped her, and was taking her to Scotland to marry her.

Her life had changed an alarming amount since this morning. Last night she had received her very first marriage proposal, and this morning she was running away to Gretna Green with an entirely different man.

'You should sleep,' he said.

'I don't think I can...'

'Sleep. Tomorrow will come quickly enough.'

It was past dawn by the time they reached Scotland. They had gone at a punishing clip, and he would need to refresh the team of horses. They would have to stay and allow his driver to rest. But it was no matter. The scandal when they arrived back in London was unavoidable. He had broken things off with Anna, and now he and Eleanor were gone. They had already missed last night's affairs, and they would not be back tonight either. He had denied Eleanor's suitor early yesterday morning...

Yes, the wheels of society would be turning already, trying to divine exactly what had happened. And they would put together the appropriate equation.

Beatrice and Briggs would likely be outraged. But it would be nice for them to try out a bit of moral

outrage for a change. He couldn't be the only one af-
flicted with it.

And where is it now?

Oh, it was there, simmering beneath the surface.
It was difficult to imagine that two days ago, he was
still everything that he had set out to be. Now he was
a debaucher of innocents and a kidnapper. It had been
a busy couple of days.

'We are here,' he said as the carriage slowed in
front of the infamous blacksmith. There was an inn
adjacent to the place, as if they knew exactly what
most couples would wish to do immediately following the hasty union.

Though he imagined, like himself and Eleanor,
most would have consummated already. Thus the
race to Scotland.

'I am in my nightclothes,' she said, sitting stub-
bornly in the carriage.

'I brought you a dress.'

'What a thoughtful rogue you are!' She looked
around. 'I'm supposed to change in here?'

'I can help.'

'No, thank you.'

'Suit yourself.' He bent down and took a dress
out of the small bag he'd packed and handed it to
her. He was thankful he'd had the forethought to do
that. There was scandal, and then there was the getting married in Scotland with the woman in a nightgown scandal.

The carriage swayed back and forth for a few minutes and then she nearly tumbled out, dressed in the claret red dress he'd packed.

'This is not appropriate for the day,' she said, her tone stiff.

'It is appropriate for anything,' he said, his voice sounding rougher than he'd intended.

He took her hand and led her across the square. It was early yet and there were few people about, but the blacksmith was there, hammering metal over an anvil. He looked up when Hugh and Eleanor approached. Hugh rather thought the two of them looked like refugees.

It was close enough to the truth.

The Duke and his ward, felled by the most basic of human sins.

Come to try and piece themselves back together with holy matrimony, the only thing that could ever truly redeem.

'Aye, you look awfully fine to be here,' the blacksmith said, looking them over.

'I will pay whatever you want,' Hugh said, feeling short-tempered.

'A dangerous offer…'

'Your Grace,' Hugh said, clipped.

'Your Grace,' the man repeated. And he grinned. And Hugh knew he would be paying much more for this wedding than most.

But he didn't have the patience for subtlety. Just as he hadn't the patience for going through the reading of the banns, or even getting a special license from the Archbishop of Canterbury, though he could have done so.

He did not want cheap and he did not want easy.

He wanted finished.

Eleanor was utterly subdued while the short ceremony took place. While they were married in a forge, over an anvil.

'How much for a room?' he asked when it was over, gesturing behind them at the inn.

'Impatient,' the blacksmith said. 'But not my inn. So you'll have to go in and ask.'

Hugh overpaid the man.

And then they walked across the dirt and he bid Eleanor wait outside in the carriage while he went into the inn.

'I suppose you didn't drive your team all night to make it to Scotland because you were interested in practising restraint. But it'll cost you.' The innkeeper grinned at him and Hugh ground his teeth together.

'I expect nothing else.'

Once he secured a room he went to fetch her from the carriage. She looked limp, her hair dishevelled, dark circles under her eyes.

They were ushered to a room that reminded him very much of the inn they had stayed at on the road to London, and he had slept on the floor to preserve her innocence and reputation. And in the time since, he had stolen both.

She looked up at him, and he could feel her exhaustion echo in his soul.

'Sleep,' he said.

'You mean you didn't… You want…'

'For God's sake, Eleanor, I am not a raving beast. We drove in the carriage all night.'

But even as he looked at her, his body went tight with need. He had been caught in the grips of some kind of madness ever since he had discovered her gone. Consumed with the idea of tying her to him. And now… He had married her.

She was his.

And truthfully, what he wanted—regardless of the sleepless night, the hours spent in the carriage— was to strip her gown off her and have her beneath him, bent over in front of him. Whatever position he could have her in, as long as he was buried deep in- side her, his throbbing manhood surrounded by her tight willing heat.

Hadn't he tortured himself with not having her for long enough?

But perhaps, just maybe, he wanted to test the last remaining shreds of his self-control.

For the sake of interest.

'I will get us food. Coffee.'

'I would like that,' she said softly.

And he looked down at the ring on her finger.

'When we get back we will begin instruction on your duties as Duchess.'

'Yes,' she said. She sat down on the edge of the bed, and she looked impossibly young, and he felt like the villain that he clearly was.

He turned and stormed out of the room, taking the

stairs two at a time as he went back down to the dining room. 'Bread and cheese. For my wife.'

His wife.

Not his ward.

His wife.

The stars.

And this time it wasn't simply to try and shield her reputation. This time it was the truth. She was his. His wife.

'And coffee,' he said.

'Didn't expect to see you resurface for a few hours,' the man said.

'I'll thank you to keep your commentary to yourself,' Hugh said.

By the time he returned to the room, Eleanor was sound asleep, lying across the bed fully dressed, her arm thrown over her face. And he felt an intense surge of protectiveness. She might not be his ward any more... But the directive had not changed. It was up to him to keep her safe. As he'd told Eleanor in the carriage, returning to England right now was out of the question. It simply couldn't happen. There would be scandal, and it needed time to die down before they returned. Needed a chance to twist into something different. And Briggs and Beatrice could help. They may be angry with him, but they clearly sided with Eleanor. So he would make some use of them yet.

He drank the coffee, left the bread and cheese for her, and left the inn. It was a short journey to the estate he owned, but it was being run with a partial staff that still saw to the upkeep of it.

He arrived and gave a list of commands along with instructions to hire more workers if they could be found. He immediately increased the wages of anyone working there.

He also had them begin working on a gourmet dinner. Something fitting for a duchess.

He went into the study and made himself right at home. He searched for paper and ink and began to draft a letter to the Duke of Brigham.

Hugh surveyed the place; it was some years since he had been here. This would be the perfect spot to ride out a bit of scandal. He and Eleanor could return in a month, finish the Season in London while everyone had time to turn their scandal into the romance of the season.

And then they would return to the country. With her as his Duchess. And they would begin the process of setting up house.

All would be well. He had managed the situation. He had been perhaps impetuous in going to Gretna Green, but he could not regret it. Not now. Not when it had all come together so nicely.

He gave the coachman who had driven him the option of returning to London or staying here. The man opted to take a horse and go back to London, and Hugh sent a letter with him that would go to Beatrice. Hugh paid him handsomely for the trouble. When he went back to the room at the inn, Eleanor was still sleeping. While she had been abed, he had accomplished quite a lot.

He walked over to the platter that was still sitting

there and pulled a chunk off the bread. The disturbance seemed to rouse her. 'Hugh?'

'If you're ready, we shall leave this place.'

'I'm not ready,' she moaned. 'I don't think I can stand more time in the carriage.'

'It will be an hour in the carriage at most. My family estate is very close to here.'

'You… You are only an hour away and we stayed in this inn?'

'I felt that you were too exhausted to carry on, and I had no way of knowing if it would be ready for us to sleep there. It is in decent shape all things considered. All of London can rest assured we are safely on honeymoon and the sharpest gossip will fade before we return.'

'How are you going to assure that the story that is told is the story you want told?'

'Briggs. Obviously.'

'I see.'

'It will give us time,' he said. She was pale. Obviously worried. He could acknowledge that perhaps there were things he could've done differently. Could've done better these past hours. 'You will not have to go and immediately assume the position of Duchess. We might have time to find our way. As husband and wife, rather than guardian and ward.'

Her cheeks went red. 'That might be… That might be best.'

'Being a duchess is demanding,' he said.

'You haven't had a duchess all this time, how demanding can it be?'

'Well, that is the issue. I have not had a duchess. And once I do, you will be expected to step into that role unquestioningly. The staff back at Bybee House know you as my ward. The staff at the London town house know you as the same.'

'And they saw. They saw you carry me through the house as you did.'

'Yes. I will not lie to you. Your fight to gain the respect of the staff may be uphill. And it isn't that I don't think you are equal to it, Eleanor, after all, you undid years of control as far as I'm concerned. But the challenge is there nonetheless.'

'You are right, of course you are. We must act with care. Which… None of this has been done with care.'

'No,' he said, his voice hard. 'I admit that. I have made mistakes and I cannot deny it.'

'Why did you kidnap me? Why didn't you wait?'

'It did not bear thinking about. I have lived my entire life trying not to be my father. Making efforts not to be the sort of man that tars everyone around me with scandal. The first broken engagement was scandal enough, though it was Penny's doing. The second… It all begins to look like my fault. And I cannot deny that this was. But the worst was seeing the way that it would rebound on Anna. Seeing the way that my behaviour is in fact not unlike my father's. I cannot pretend that it isn't. I was self-seeking in my behaviour with you. And then… With that engagement broken… The only thing I could think of was finding you and binding you to me as quickly as possible. Leaving no more room for anything else. Noth-

ing more to negotiate on. Nothing more to discuss.
Society could disapprove as vocally as they choose,
but if we are already married, then there is nothing
to be done. And I wanted to ensure that was the case.
But I did not consider that it would be announcing
our transgressions.'

'But alas.'

He chuckled. 'Alas.'

'I am wearing a ballgown,' she said.

'Yes. We will… We will fix that. When we get to
the estate.'

'But I have to get there.'

'You married me in front of a blacksmith in the
ballgown. There's no real use being upset about it
now.'

'My debut as Duchess will be in this?'

'You are resplendent.'

'I feel…'

She was uncomfortable. And it did not matter what
he thought. She did not think the gown was suitable
for the country during the day and perhaps she was
right.

He would fix it.

All that he had broken, he would fix.

He left her again and returned not long after, having purchased clothing from the blacksmith that he
was fairly certain belonged to the man's wife.

A dark green dress made of a serviceable fabric
that would not have been remotely fashionable in
London.

He did not turn away as she changed. This time, he

watched as the diaphanous fabric fell to the floor, and she quickly pulled up the other garment. He went behind her and began to do up the laces. And he felt her shift in discomfort. 'I'm your husband now,' he said.

'I'm still not sure how to feel about it.'

'You don't have to know,' he said. 'It simply is.'

'That is an incredibly arrogant thing to say.'

'I am incredibly arrogant, if you had not yet figured it out.'

In all his fantasies, he had not thought of putting Eleanor back in her clothes. But there was a strange sort of intimacy to it. He had taken care of her these many years, but never in this fashion. Never directly.

He finished with the dress, then moved his hands down her back, and she gasped, turning to face him, her eyes wide.

'I...'

'Let us go,' he said.

He took her hand, and the sensation nearly undid him. She was so soft.

And he could hold her hand if he wished. She was his wife. Not his ward.

They walked out of the bedroom together and went down the stairs. He could feel her shrink against him, and he was more pleased than he should be that she clung to him. That she could.

He approached the innkeeper, who stood behind the bar.

'Please see that any of our remaining things are packed up and brought to the estate,' Hugh said as they prepared to leave the inn. 'I will pay handsomely.'

'Yes, Your Grace,' the man said.

Hugh helped Eleanor into the carriage outside. She turned and looked out of the window as the carriage rolled out of the village and into the countryside, where the estate stood, all stacked grey stone with the intense green of Scotland behind.

'We are staying here?'

'It is our home,' he said. 'For whenever we wish to return to it. For this next measure of time.'

'How long, do you suppose?'

'I will have Briggs keep me informed of the situation back in London.'

'Hugh, I have to ask. What of Anna? You are leaving her there to deal with this fallout alone.'

'It is better. The gossip about us will fly. And she is free to handle it however she sees fit.' He had, after all, as much as admitted to her that he had ruined Eleanor. 'I do not think my presence would aid things.'

'Perhaps not,' Eleanor said.

'You are genuinely concerned about her?' Hugh asked.

'Yes. I am. She is a woman, and this world is unforgiving of us. She is not my rival, and she never was. I wanted you, it's true. But I had accepted that I could not have you in this way. I knew that she was right. I knew that she was right to be your Duchess.'

'I must ask you, Eleanor, because you seemed so surprised when I proposed marriage. What did you think would happen? What did you think my intentions were when I carried you up the stairs?'

She looked straight ahead, her face pale. 'I had decided that I would accept a life as your mistress.'

He frowned. 'And you thought…'

'I had nothing else to think. You know as well as I that I am unsuitable. And if you were a different man… Maybe even Briggs, I would not have thought that to be such a barrier. But I know how you feel about your father. I know what this is doing to you. I know. And you must understand that it was a fate that I feared more than anything. But I expected that it would be mine.'

'You were prepared to live life like that, in the margins, to be with me?'

It was the cake. All over again. Except… It could not even really be compared. She had given herself to him with no expectations at all. In fact, she had given herself to him thinking the very worst of him.

'I didn't see another choice. I couldn't fight it any more. And I didn't want to.'

'But then you ran from me?'

She turned to him, her expression grave. 'I had accepted that I share you with her. I knew that she had to be your Duchess. And I did not hate her for that. I thought… I'd live in my house and she in hers. She with you. My children could share my home with me, and you could share my bed when you wished. And it all seemed like a certain sort of happiness. I convinced myself in the time between your kiss in the garden to the moment you carried me up the stairs that it would all be all right. But when it was done I knew. I thought I knew everything about the intimacy between a man and a woman, Hugh, because I knew what the physical actions were. But I did not understand. Not really. When it was over, I knew that I could not bear to have you touch another woman. To have you live with another woman. To have you give her children while ours had to be barely acknowledged and...'

'But it is not our fate,' he said, reaching out and touching her face. 'It is not what we are.'

Her eyes filled with tears. 'I could scarcely believe it. Truly I cannot.'

'Come into your home, my Duchess. Perhaps then it will feel more real.'

Chapter Seventeen

Eleanor was a woman in a world built for men. Nothing that had been called hers had ever been bought with money belonging to her, money that she had earned. Not a single stitch of clothing. And none of it had ever truly belonged to her. No place she had ever lived, no bed she had ever slept in.

And it was not any different now that she had been given the title. But it felt different. When she was a ward everything that surrounded her had been so easily lost. But now she was the Duchess of Kendal. And everything that was Hugh's she had indirect ownership of as well. A say in the running of things, authority when it came to the staff.

And when she crossed the threshold of that house, it all hit her.

Everything had changed. She had thought only wildly, ridiculously, that she and Hugh could be together again. And it had been hours now since they had married and he had yet to kiss her. To strip her naked.

All of it had seemed to be about that. It was why they had come here, after all. That failure of self-control. That desperate need to be with one another. It was why they were here at all. And so this… This had all seemed secondary. She had been thinking in terms of her and him. Of the man and woman they were. But the man he was could not be separated from the fact that he was the Duke of Kendal. That he was power-ful. That on a whim he had taken her to his estate in the countryside of Scotland because he did not wish to subject her to gossip.

That he did so with ease, without thought, was something she could only marvel at.

'Whatever you wish to have done here, you have only to say. I have taken the liberty of beginning the week's menu for us, as I thought that might be easi-est for you. From here on, however, that will be your responsibility.'

'I get to choose what we eat?'

She had never had such authority. The tables that she sat at contained food that was not hers either, and she could only ever be grateful for what had been pre-pared. If sometimes something happened to be a par-ticular favourite, then it was all the better. But to have the authority to choose what went on the menus…

'Yes.'

'Hugh, I cannot fathom it,' she said, feeling peril-ously close to weeping again.

'You were planning on marrying…did you not think of the ways in which you might run a household?

'I was terrified that I would not actually marry. I

thought only of securing the proposal and then… I did not expect ever to marry a man so fine as you.'

He looked at her, long and hard, his face granite. 'Do you mean the sense of my title, or the quality of my character?'

'I meant your title,' she said. She swallowed hard. 'And I never thought of marrying you. Because it was a madness to even consider it.'

But it was a lie. She had thought of it. She had dreamed it.

But girls like her did not get their dreams. And she could not now orient to the fact that she was standing in the middle of one.

That she was standing in the stars.

All that was impossible was right here. Perfectly within her reach. All these things. All this freedom. All this choice. But most of all him. They could go to his bedchamber alone. He could see her body. And she could see his. Society no longer owned the relationship between them. They did. What he wanted to do with her was entirely his affair, and that which she desired to do with him was hers.

Her body. Her needs. Her desires. All of them had belonged to the people around them more than they had ever belonged to her. Her behaviour had been dictated by people she didn't even personally know, let alone care about. And they no longer owned her. He did, it was true, but in that ownership, she was set free.

Because the truest freedom that she desired was

that to be found in his bed. And she had the authority to claim it.

'Where are the servants?'

'Scrambling, I imagine,' he said. 'I have given quite a long list of orders for things to be prepared.'

She looked around, and then took a step towards him, pressing her fingertips to his lips, letting them drift to the corner of his mouth. He closed his eyes as she smoothed her thumb over his rough stubble and jaw. 'Hugh…'

He wrapped his hand around her wrist, his grip iron, and he pulled her up against him, lowering his head and kissing her with a ferocity that took her breath away.

'My wife,' he said, rubbing his nose against hers, and she really did think she might swoon.

'I do not even remember where the bedchamber is, but I will find it.'

He picked her up, and she found herself being carried up the stairs again, but this was different. This was different. They were married. She was his wife.

And she wanted to weep with the joy of it.

He walked down the corridor and pushed the door open. There were two maids, leaning over a large bed, just finishing with blankets. 'Thank you,' Hugh said. 'That will be all.'

The girls looked at each other, and then scurried out with barely suppressed laughter, and Eleanor fought the surge of embarrassment that rushed to her cheeks.

She had nothing to be embarrassed about. Yes,

they knew exactly what was about to happen in this room. But if they were married to a man who looked like him, they would be eager to do the same thing. Of that she thought there could be no doubt.

He shut the door with decisive ferocity and began to tear at the laces on the back of her gown that he had only just done up. 'How helpful for me that I have an intimate understanding of how this dress was put on. For I know all the better how to take it off. But it is that crimson gown…'

'You love that dress,' she said.

'I do,' he said. 'Every single dress that you got for the Season has been a torment to me. A rainbow of all that I could not have. But the red most of all. I saw you and that meant… You could not have been more unsuitable for me. And maybe that was why I wanted you. You were temptation incarnate, and so innocent with it. Eleanor, you have no idea what it is you do to me. I do not know myself for wanting you. All these years, I thought that I knew what drove me. I thought that I knew what I wanted. All of it was obliterated by the view of you in that dress.'

He undressed her with haste, left her nude, and she was not embarrassed.

He consigned his coat to the floor, his shirt, his breeches. And she couldn't take her eyes off him. She gazed on every lean, perfectly honed inch. On that most masculine part of him that had already been inside her once, and that she ached to be filled with again.

It had hurt, that first time. And even if it hurt again,

she would take him gladly. She found she was grateful to not be so wholly innocent now. To have this moment where it wasn't all desperation and pain. There was desire, but they had all the time in the world. She no longer felt like they were racing against the clock that was ticking down the minutes against them.

No longer felt as if she was racing against the moment of clarity that she had been certain would come for him if he had even a second to think.

The time for clarity had passed. And they were married now.

And she could not get over it. That she had spent so many years denying herself the need for him, and now here they were. Naked together.

When she had tried hard for so long to not even drink in the intimate details of his face. The way his clothes shaped to his masculine physique. And now she was looking at him without those clothes.

'I do not know what I am allowed to do,' she said, feeling shy suddenly.

'Anything,' he said. His expression was raw, his voice rough. 'I will admit to you, Eleanor, that I am not an innocent. Far from it. I have tried always to keep my liaisons with women confined to appropriate places, and you are the first that I have ever violated that with. I was never with Anna. Not like this. With her I would've waited for marriage. With her I was not tested. I did not want her.'

'I don't wish to hear about you with other women,' she said.

'I can understand that. I would not wish to hear about you with other men.'

'You know there has been no other man. Not even a kiss.'

He made a low, satisfied sound in the back of his throat. 'I am far happier about that than I should be.'

'Hugh,' she said. 'Why are you telling me about other women?'

'Because I wish you to understand, that I have explored desire in great detail, with women who make it their profession. And there is nothing that can shock me. I worry that I might shock you. This is the problem, Eleanor. I did not wish to marry a woman I had a great deal of passion for.'

'Why?'

'Because I wish to keep vices where vices go. I did not ever wish to be my father, with things spilling into each other, mixing and causing destruction. But now I have done the ultimate, haven't I? Taken my ward as my own. Your father…'

'I think that my father would be all right with what has occurred, considering that you married me. But you made me a duchess. I know that he never had designs on that.'

'I know he did not. Eleanor, the things that I want to do to you are not fitting for a man to do to his wife.'

'Why not?'

'Because a man treats his wife like a lady. Not like a whore.'

The words, spoken as if they were entirely separate entities, made her feel extremely uncomfortable.

'That seems to imply that a man would have need of a whore, even after his marriage. I had been told this. That it was the function of mistresses to serve a man's appetites. I was prepared to be your mistress. I was prepared to be what satiated your desire when your wife could not. But now I am your wife. So allow me to be both. Allow me to be everything. Let there be no limits between us so that there is never a need for another. Please.'

Fire flared in his gaze. 'What a pretty picture you make, saying *please* naked before me. The only thing that could be more beautiful was if you were on your knees.'

And so she dropped to her knees, then and there, her hands widespread. 'Please.'

The flame in his eyes rose higher, his nostrils flaring. That most masculine part of him left with his need for her. And he moved to where she knelt, putting his hand on the back of her head and stroking her. And she was close, so close to his male member, her heart thundering hard. Tentatively, she reached out and wrapped her fingers around his thick, hard shaft. He growled low and hard. Hugh. She was touching him like this. And he was tested for his control, not because he was angry, but because he desired her.

'I have no right…'

'Let me be everything. Your wife. Your ward. Your mistress.'

'Eleanor…' She tested his strength, squeezing him until he shuddered. 'Is that all right?'

'Your mouth,' he said. 'Use your mouth on me.'

And she didn't understand how she would. But she wanted to. That rough command sent an explosion of heat rioting through her body, and she grew wet between her thighs. She knew what that meant now. She remembered how he had been able to thrust inside of her, aided by that wetness. Her body was preparing itself for him. Her body desired this.

And even if she didn't understand why, or how, she knew that she wanted it. She leaned in, and pressed a kiss to his shaft. Treating it as she might his mouth. And what always happened after that first press of his lips. He opened his mouth. And so she opened hers, taking the tip inside, careful not to skim her teeth over him.

He cursed, short and harsh, his fingers shoved deep into her hair, tugging. 'Yes,' he said, broken. She looked up at him, and his eyes met hers, an impossible fire burning inside her. To feel as if he was watching her do this to him, to feel so seen by him, it was impossibly arousing, and she could not explain it. So she took him in deeper, her eyes still on his as she did.

He cursed again as she did her best to swallow him, inch by inch. Though it was an impossibility to take all of him given his size. He guided her movements then, tugging and releasing his hold on her hair as she teased them both. He tasted musky, salty, and she loved the intimacy of it.

The power that she felt here.

She no longer felt as if the world belonged to everyone but her. He was hers. In this moment, he was hers, and there was no questioning it. And it made her feel strong. It made her feel like for once she wasn't simply a burden. But that she could give. And she wanted to. She wanted to give him everything. She pleasured him like that until he was shaking. Until he wrenched her head away from him, leaving her scalp stinging. Then he picked her up and carried her to the bed, laid her down across it, with her bottom on the end of the mattress. And he knelt before her. Her Duke. And put his face between her thighs. He licked her, decisively, deeply, and she held onto his hair as he had just done to her, a slave to the sensation that he was pouring over her.

His mouth was hot and slick and firm. His movements decisive. And she whimpered, her hips rolling upward to meet his questing tongue. He pushed a finger inside of her, and then another, raw and without quarter. He pleasured her until she was sobbing, until release burst within her midsection and left her panting and pleading with him to stop.

But he didn't. He sucked her into his mouth, like she was dessert, and she shattered yet again.

'Hugh,' she begged.

'Not until I say,' he said. 'You must be mindless for me.'

'I am,' she said.

'My woman will want nothing else. And no one else. You will never be in doubt of who you belong to.'

He moved up her body like a predatory cat, his blue eyes intense on hers as he braced himself on the mattress and looked down. 'Mine,' he said, putting his hand between her legs and teasing her as he said it.

'Yes,' she said.

'You were going to marry that boy. Take his cock inside of you. You were going to do that.'

'I didn't know,' she said.

'You will never want another man's cock. Do you understand?'

'I don't. I won't.'

'Who do you belong to?'

'You,' she said. And then he thrust inside her, filling her ruthlessly. 'Your Grace,' she gasped, letting her head fall back, her chest arching up off the mattress, and he lowered his head, taking one nipple between his teeth, biting her.

'Hugh,' she gasped.

She tried to grab his shoulders, but he took her wrists in his hand, pinning them roughly above her head as he thrust into her, so hard they were no longer at the edge of the mattress, rather they were hitting up against the headboard as he claimed her with each invasion of her body. 'Hugh,' she whimpered his name, over and over again as he pounded into her relentlessly.

She wrapped her legs around his waist, which allowed him to go deeper, and she began to shake, the climax that built inside her starting from somewhere so impossibly deep she hadn't known existed. And it began to build, growing slowly, growing outward, taking her senses along with it. She trembled, shook, and when her need claimed her she could only cry out his name. And then he broke, whispering her name against her breastbone as he poured himself inside of her.

And this time, he didn't sleep. This time he held her against his body, and she ran her hands over his chest, down to his thigh and back up again. She explored him, never stopping, restless hunger gnawing at her even as she did. She felt exhausted. She didn't think it would be possible for her to ever reach her peak again, and yet impossibly... She wanted him.

Her fingertips drifted over his... The part of him that had just been inside her.

'You must give me a moment,' he said.

'Does it take time?'

'For men? Yes. With you? Less time than usual.'

'I ache for you,' she said.

'You're insatiable,' he said, but he looked pleased at the thought.

And she was glad.

She rolled over onto her side and looked at him. There had always been a barrier between the two of them.

How could there not be?

There had been many, in point of fact. She was part of the household, and yet not. He was her superior in rank. He was a man. And he was her guardian. And here they were, equal in this moment. Both of them naked and spent. No more propriety observed between them at all. He had said words to her that she had never heard spoken in polite company, or any company for that matter. He had tasted her and touched her in places she had never imagined any man would, let alone him.

And she… She had done the same to him.

He was very intense like this.

But then, he was always intense. But she had not thought that… He was a man who seemed so obsessed with propriety. And yet he was in no way inhibited in his play. He was not light. But he was not the sort of man who acted with any sort of restraint either.

'I do not understand you,' she said.

'In what way?' he asked.

'You try so hard to do everything… You are a man who prizes doing the right thing in the eyes of society. And I understand why. I understand how your father was. But you are not… I do not know overmuch about the way men are with their wives. But you are not what I would expect either.'

'It has always been my great shame that my appetite is voracious. And… It has long been the only place that I could ever…' He looked at her, his expression strained. 'I am rough, Eleanor. I should not be rough with you. And yet I find that I do not think when I see you. There is only desire. And everything that I have ever done or ever wanted to do with another woman… None of it will ever truly mean anything until it's with you. All of that was simply wasting time.'

'And what is it you like?'

'I told you. I like to leave marks. It makes me feel…' She could see he was reaching deep for an answer, and that he feared she would be repulsed by his admission.

She understood.

She simply did.

'Like what you've done meant something. Like it lasted.' She put her hand on his mouth, and traced his lips with the tip of her finger. 'Has anyone ever thanked you?'

'For their climax?'

She laughed. And she saw that he was quite serious. 'No. Not for that. Though they were very nice. Did they ever thank you for what you did for Beatrice? Has Beatrice ever thanked you? The weight that you carried in the household... And you became the Duke so young. Has anyone ever thanked you for all that you have done to put the family back together in the wake of your father's scandals? Or does it sometimes feel like you work and work and carry everything, and no one knows. It must feel good to do something that you can leave your fingerprints behind on.'

His eyes widened fractionally for a moment, and then his mouth firmed into a thin line. 'I...'

'I have belonged to no one except you for a very long time. And I know that I was never meant to belong to you in this way. But everything felt temporary. Like I was passing through, until I could be handed off. And I want nothing more than for the impressions of your fingers to be left behind on my skin. I want for nothing more than to feel your hold long after you have stopped clinging to me. I would take your pain and your pleasure, because it will make me feel like this is real. Like it isn't a dream. Like it isn't simply a moment that will pass. Hugh, I would take any pleasure from you. Any pain. If only it meant that I could be yours. For real.'

'I will never betray you. I promise that. I will never do to you what my father did to my mother.'

'I know. I do.' She leaned against him and pressed her lips to his chest. 'Thank you. Without you, I would have nothing. I would be nothing.'

He said nothing, but he put his hand on her shoulder, and moved his thumb in slow circles against her bare skin. It was the middle of the day, but she wanted to sleep. And she felt so safe lying in his arms, that she decided to do just that.

Chapter Eighteen

The letter that came from Briggs two days later made it very clear that the scandal had erupted after their departure. But Hugh could not see his way around that. And he didn't much care. Perhaps it was because after the wonderful dinner he had last night, he had taken his wife to bed and made love to her at least three more times before exhaustion had claimed them.

She had met with the household staff and planned the menu for the rest of the week. She was getting a taste of what it would mean to be a duchess when they went back to London, and when they returned to run the country estate, Bybee House.

It would be more difficult there. The servants would know her already. But she would weather it fine. She was already brilliant at running things here. Or perhaps he was just well satisfied. Either way, it did not matter. It was a strange sensation, having that which he had craved for so long and denied himself. He was not a man who was given to self-gratification.

It was a novel experience.

He had to wonder if this was how his father had felt all the time.

He shoved that thought to the side. And he finished his correspondence to Briggs. He left his study and went downstairs, and found a small boy working in the boot room. 'A letter for London,' he said. 'Take this to a mail coach.'

The boy grinned, and took the coin Hugh offered, scampering off. He could hear Eleanor's voice coming from the drawing room, and he followed the sound of it, momentarily left breathless when he walked in and saw her talking to the housekeeper.

Her blonde hair was pinned up, a sedate pink dress making her cheeks look extra rosy.

She was the picture of propriety, and he could only see the potential for debauchery.

Now that the pretence was removed… He simply wanted her. Always.

'Your Grace,' the housekeeper said, nodding in his direction. 'Your Grace,' she said to Eleanor.

Eleanor smiled, and gave the woman a small wave as she left.

'I think we have sorted out the provisions for the week,' Eleanor said, smiling.

'Good,' he said. But he did not think that he could concentrate on any sort of hunger for food when the dominant hunger he felt was for her.

And he realised he did not have to practise any restraint at all. She was his wife. And this was his home. He shut the drawing room door and locked it firmly.

'What are you…'

'You look so perfectly respectable, every inch the sort of woman that I would marry.'

'Yes?'

'It has aroused me so much, I wish to make you look as disreputable as possible.' He wouldn't be like this when they went back to London. This would just be here. Here, where they were away from everyone and everything. Here, where the spectre of his father didn't loom quite so large.

How he wanted her. It was unlike anything he had ever experienced before. Perhaps it was all too familiar. Because hadn't he wanted her like this for far too long? Hadn't he craved her in ways that were debauched and indecent from the moment she had become a woman? If his honour were pinned on this very thing, then he had no honour left. And he knew it.

But he didn't care now. Because she was his. His. He could have her anytime he wanted to. Have her in the middle of the day. In this drawing room. In that dress, out of that dress. He could have whatever he wanted.

He was a duke, after all.

And suddenly, he felt enraged. Enraged that he had ever denied himself anything. He had been born into a position that allowed him to demand whatever he wished. He had allowed his father to dictate how far he could go. But he did not have a wife. At least, he had not. He had taken this woman for his wife now, and what was the purpose in denying himself?

It was only so that he could say that he was better than his father.

And who cared? Anna had assumed that he had debauched Eleanor already, when he had done no such thing. Likely, everyone assumed it, and no one had dared speak it. So why not? Why not have absolutely everything?

Her pulse was pounding hard at the base of her throat and he felt an answering throb in his cock. He moved his hand down to the front of his breeches and adjusted himself, unable to resist the urge to squeeze himself to alleviate some of the roaring need that was prowling through his body like a lion. Her eyes were fixed on his hand, on his movement. And he could see that pulse flutter faster.

Unable to stop himself, he extended his hand, and placed it there, covering her pulse. She shuddered, a little moan of delight escaping her lips as he put a possessive hand around her neck. This was something he'd always found erotic, though not something he often did. It frightened him, the ferocity of the feelings that it aroused in him. And it had never seemed like anything he wanted to visit on the women he paid to warm his bed. But he was driven now. Because there was something about the power in it. And the trust. That she would allow him to hold her like this.

She moaned her pleasure at the possessive hold.

It was more than allowing him to do this.

She wanted it.

He let his fingers drift down to the neckline of her gown, teasing the lace edge there, teasing her skin.

'I will have you naked beneath me in here. In this room where you were only just planning your menu. That is being my wife, and my mistress. What do you think about that?'

'It pleases me,' she said.

'Good. That means you will run my household, and you will see to my needs. And you will do both happily.'

'Yes.'

She was shaking with her desire for him, and it sent a shock of need through him that defied anything he had ever known.

He rather liked the gown. But it was not the red gown, and he did not care for its preservation. He wrapped his fingers around the neckline and tore it down.

'Oh,' she breathed.

'There will be more coming from London. From Paris. I will give you everything. Everything you could ever desire will be yours. Beautiful gowns, antiquities to fill the house, jewellery. Whatever you want. You are mine, and I will mark you as such. There will not be any doubt that you are the wife of the Duke of Kendal. No other woman will be as fine as you.'

He saw something shimmer in her eyes, but he could not quite put a name to it.

He didn't want to. This was his fantasy. And she was his.

He pushed her skirts up past her hips, exposing her to him, that pale, glorious heart of her, pink and damp with her need for him. And he lifted her up and set her on a side table, parting her thighs as wide as they would go, examining that shining cleft. He was so hard it was a physical pain. But he didn't care. This was what he wanted. She was what he wanted.

He opened the front of his breeches and released his throbbing arousal, guiding himself to the heart of her before teasing the entrance to her body with his already damp head. Then he pushed it through her folds, drawing it over that sensitive bundle of nerves at her cleft until she was shaking. Shivering. She let her head fall back, exposing her throat, and he wrapped his fingers around her, squeezing hard. She moaned and arched her hips towards him, beseeching. 'Look at me,' he commanded. Her eyes opened wide, and she stared at him, a dreamy look on her face as he rammed himself inside her, tightening his hold on her neck.

This was no sweet coupling in their bed, no leisurely afternoon playtime. He was driven by the intense need to claim her. To mark her as his.

To luxuriate in the fact that he pleasured her, and she allowed him to take her in hand in a way that left her so vulnerable.

And yet she did so joyfully.

His. His to care for. And she thanked him.

These burdens had been on him all his life, and he had not chosen a single one. But he cared for every responsibility that was given to him. But nothing was truly for him. He was a steward of whatever it was on behalf of someone else. It was true even of his title.

And Eleanor most of all, when she had been his

ward. He had been caring for her until she would be given to another. But now... Now she was his wife. His wife.

His.

He increased the strength of his thrusts, his hold, and as the colour rose in her cheeks, the intensity rose in him. She cried out, a short and sharp breath, and he could feel her internal muscles rippling around him. She was so wet, so needy that it made it nearly impossible for him to hold himself back.

But he wanted this to go on. He had never wanted to live in a moment quite like this. Not once in his life. But he wanted to stay in this, in her, for ever.

'Eleanor,' he ground out.

And then she shattered, breathy sighs escaping her mouth as she clamped down hard on him, forcing his own climax to a head. He roared, spilling his seed inside her and releasing hold of her, bracing himself on the table, resting his head against the crook of her neck. He kissed her there. Kissed her on every red indentation left behind by his fingers. She wrapped her arms around him, held his head there. And he felt suddenly exposed. Because had he not known this woman since she was a girl? Had she not known him since he was a young, green boy? And now she knew these things about him. These dark, terrible things. The things that drove him to claim, mark, possess. And none half so intense as what drove him with her. He had been with strangers before. Women who accepted money for the privilege of being in their bodies.

This was not the same. She was not the same.

'Hugh, that...'

'I'm sorry,' he said, drawing away. 'I was unforgivably rough.'

'No,' she said. 'Why would you say that when we've already agreed that there is nothing between the two of us that is not accepted happily.'

Because he wanted to hide from her, and this was the perfect reason to do it. Because he should feel guilty for what he had done. It was only that he did not.

'There was no excuse for me to not obtain your permission. And establish a word.'

'A word?'

'Something you can say if anything becomes too difficult for you to bear.'

'Hugh, if I had said stop, you would have done so.'

And he realised this was true. He knew another word was customary, particularly if it was a game where the men enjoyed being told to stop and not stopping. But that was not his game. And had she acted in distress at all, he would not have continued.

'But I should have...'

'I am happy,' she said. 'I'm happy with you. I'm a little bit less happy that you tore my dress, because it was quite a nice dress. But you do not need to apologise to me for what I did willingly.' A strange little smile crossed her face. 'Is that what you meant when I threatened to choke you?'

He had forgotten entirely what she was talking about. 'What?'

'In the carriage on the way to London. You said you do not allow women to do the choking.'

'I did not think you liked to hear about my exploits with other women.'

'I'm trying to understand you. And maybe in order to do so I need to hear something that I may not particularly like.'

'It is something that I have enjoyed. Yes. It is the ultimate possession to me. But I do not… That is not typical. What passed between us just now was unique. Being inside of you while I held you like that. It made me feel like you were mine. Wholly and deeply. You were not afraid, were you?'

'No. No, it made me feel powerful. Because that hold would have been dangerous, if you were anyone else. If I were anyone else. And I might have been afraid, but I wasn't. Because the two of us are safe for each other. I am strong enough for you. You are exactly what I need. No one has ever wanted me like you. I am happy to be yours. I'm glad that you wish to… To hold me so.'

And he was stripped even more raw than he had been a moment ago. How was it that she understood? It was something he could not understand. Because he didn't understand the things that drove him.

He did not understand why he sought relief in the way that he did. And yet she seemed to. The way that she would reflect his thoughts back to him, as if it all made perfect sense. It was something that he could not quite comprehend. The way she did that.

The way she simply understood.

It undid him.

'We are having a very lovely chicken for dinner,' she said.

And he laughed. He couldn't help it. He laughed at the absurdity of it all, because what else could he do? And he thought dimly that Eleanor was the only person to have made him laugh in longer than he could remember, and she had done it twice.

'What do you find so amusing?'

'You really have managed to be both my wife and my mistress, quite neatly in the space of the last few moments.'

'And what does that make you to me? My husband and my master?'

The word made him shiver, somewhere down deep. 'Perhaps just Hugh,' he said.

'Not Your Grace?'

'You may call me that if you wish. I particularly like it when you are on your knees.'

It was true. Though he could not say why.

'Then I will be sure to do that. After we have our lovely roast chicken for dinner.' She sighed. 'Now you have to work out how to get me out of here without compromising what little is left of my decency.'

'You are everything decent and good,' he said, and he meant that.

'I think we both know I am not. What sort of decent, good woman allows those sorts of things to go on in the middle of the day, in the drawing room. We will never be able to entertain in here. The spectre of what we just did will echo in my mind and when anyone sets a tea cup on that table I will remember when you set me on the table.'

'We will not entertain much here.'

This place would be for the two of them. And London waited.

And...

Well, his mother. He had not yet written to his mother, but he imagined Beatrice would have. And he had a feeling he would be receiving an irate letter any day...

She would be very cross that she'd missed his wedding.

But she would be furious over what he'd done to Anna.

And what he'd done to Eleanor. Eleanor may not realise it yet but this was no fantasy.

She was happy to be married, and he could understand that, given what her fears had been.

But she didn't know him.

Not truly.

When they returned to their real lives in England, they would have different roles to fill than they did here.

But until then, he would indulge himself with his bride.

That seemed a fair gift to give himself.

Chapter Nineteen

She would have stayed in Scotland for ever.

She had never known life like this before, and she had never even known to dream of it. Here she was different, and yet, more herself than she'd ever been.

She chose what to eat. She chose what to wear—clothes had appeared as if by magic, so truth be told she was choosing from a selection curated by someone else, but she was not on display here so it was different from life in London or even life at Bybee House.

She did not think about pleasing anyone but herself.

She hoped that she pleased Hugh, but she did not worry about it.

She no longer felt like she was in peril. Balancing her desires with her fate on the edge of a knife.

Today she ran out in the fields like a child. It was cold, the sky grey, the wind biting, but she didn't mind. She'd spent the day exploring the grounds while Hugh saw to correspondence in his study.

She missed him when he had to attend to other

duties. Which was a foolish thing to think. He was here. Right here with her.

But perhaps it was simply that it reminded her of life before this.

This felt protected. This felt like it might be a fantasy, and maybe that was why when he had to slip into his role as the Duke of Kendal, even here in their oasis, she felt slightly ill at ease.

Here, she felt free.

But she couldn't imagine bringing this level of freedom back to their lives in England.

It would be impossible. They would be pushed into roles again.

But now she would be his wife and not his ward, and what did that mean?

She had no idea. So she ran across the fields and embraced the freedom that came with it.

She heard the sound of a horse's hooves and stopped, then turned to see a black steed racing towards her.

There was no doubt as to who rode on his back.

Hugh was a dashing figure on a horse. She'd discovered she had a particular weakness for that years ago.

She could remember clearly the first time she'd been affected by it. She'd been maybe thirteen and she'd seen him riding across the lawn at Bybee House, his black coat billowing behind him, his strong thighs gripping the horse with a level of strength and mastery that had made her stomach feel like it was trembling.

She hadn't known what that feeling was, not then.

But she understood it now, and it was no less for having been with the man intimately. If anything, it was more intense now. Because she knew.

He lived up to every fantasy she could have ever woven about him.

'I didn't expect to find a damsel in distress while out on my ride,' he said.

'You didn't,' she responded. 'You found a damsel perfectly happy with her own company.'

'I can go.'

'No. Please. Stay.' Her heart bumped in her chest, and she felt foolish for asking him to stay as she had. She sounded desperate. She was desperate.

He manoeuvred his horse around to her and reached his hand down. She took it and let him lift her up onto the back of the horse with ease—he was truly so strong, and she'd now been lifted, thrown and carried by him many times—settling her in front of him on the horse.

His hard thighs rested on either side of hers, his chest strong and hot behind her back.

And he urged the horse forward, and they went, like lightning.

She wasn't an accomplished rider. In fact, she barely rode at all, and this experience—being astride the horse and pressed against him while they went so quickly—was like the very perfect picture of all that they were here.

Fast, and brilliant, exciting and new.

Everything she had never known she wanted.

Dirt and grass flung up behind them as the horse

tore through the landscape, through the fields and to a grove of trees at the other side.

She was breathless by the time they got there, laughing.

'Care to sit for a picnic?' he asked.

'A picnic?'

'I brought some food, nothing too exciting.'

'How did you know I was out here?'

'I was looking for you. I was told you were somewhere on the grounds.'

'You were looking for me?' she asked, peering over her shoulder at his face.

A smile curved the corner of his mouth and for a moment he almost looked…like a mere man, and not the imposing Duke. 'I will always look for you.'

Her breath seemed to evaporate.

'I will always wish to be found.'

He got off the horse first, then helped her to the ground. In his hold, she floated. He opened up a pack on the side of the horse and took out bread wrapped in cloth, cheese and a bottle of wine.

'An afternoon indulgence,' he said.

'More clothed than our usual,' she said.

'I would not strip you naked out here, we are likely to be caught by one of the shepherds.'

The idea of that made her cheeks go hot.

'We must travel back to England,' he said. 'Tomorrow.'

'Tomorrow? Why?' She wanted to argue. To tell him no. But he was her husband, and he was the Duke, and even with that humour lurking around his mouth, she could see that lack of compromise there too.

'Briggs has informed me the gossip won't get better until we return, in his opinion. He thinks the initial wave has passed and now we need to show ourselves. There is a particular ball in two days... We should be there.'

'Then we will return. Whatever you need, I'm here for you.'

And he looked at her then as if he was looking at something rare. Something he had never seen before. She had to wonder if anyone had ever offered him anything. Hugh had cared for them. All of them. For all these years. But no one had ever cared for him. She purposed then, that whatever else her role as Duchess involved, she would do that.

She would be there for him. Always.

The journey back to London was markedly different from the journey away, which had been made under the cover of darkness, and with extreme haste, and with things tense and uncertain between them.

She was his wife now.

When they arrived back at his London town house, it was evening, and it felt quite different to when they had first arrived at the house in Scotland.

In Scotland he had been a different man than she'd ever known him to be. In Scotland, he'd been Hugh.

Here, he was the Duke, and she sensed...she knew, it would be different.

That he would be different.

From the moment he'd arrived and kidnapped her it had been clear something in him had unravelled. All that control.

But it was back in place now. Firmly.

It made her sad, even though she knew it was simply the way it had to be.

'You are the Duchess of Kendal,' he said. 'And no one is to make you feel inferior.'

She smiled at him, but he could see that the smile was a struggle. He took her arm, and they walked into the town house. He could feel the hush that fell over the household.

'Did you not receive word that I would be back?' he asked the butler.

'We did, Your Grace. My apologies. Everyone is of course eager to see you with your new bride.'

'They all know my bride,' he said.

'Of course.'

And that was all that was spoken on the subject.

He realised that all of Eleanor's things were in her room. That was of course how things were normally done. The Duchess would have her own room. It did, however, seem strange to put her right back in the same room she had been in before.

And yet, there was no practical purpose to moving her.

'The rest of the Duchess's clothing arrived while you were away,' his valet told him as they readied him for dinner.

'I assume her lady's maid has informed her of this?'

'Yes, Your Grace,' he said.

'I imagine you find it unusual I did not send for you while I was in Scotland,' Hugh said.

'Unless you were associating with high society, Your Grace, then I do not. In any case, it is not my place to find anything you do strange.'

'But do you?'

'Unexpected, possibly. Strange, no.'

And Hugh decided not to press for any more information. If the man thought it not at all strange because he found Eleanor beautiful, then Hugh did not need to know that. And if he found it not at all strange because he had been aware of Hugh's attraction to his ward the entire time, then he did not need to know that either.

There was a sharp rap on the door and Hugh bade the knocker enter. 'The Duke of Brigham has sent word that he should like yourself and the Duchess to join him for dinner,' the servant said.

'Send word back that we will be there,' Hugh said. Because he could not reject the invitation of his brother-in-law, particularly not as they were the keepers of all the information that Hugh and Eleanor would need for going out tomorrow night.

'Make sure the Duchess gets word as well.'

When he finished getting ready, he stood at the bottom of the stairs, waiting for Eleanor. It reminded him very much of the time before they had become husband and wife. Had it only been a month? It was nearly unbelievable that things had changed so much in that span of time.

And when she appeared at the top of the stairs,

it was in a rich emerald green that tightened his gut and set him on fire.

Her pale skin seemed highlighted by the rich colour, the roses in her cheeks and lips seeming that much more pronounced. Her blonde hair was arranged in an elaborate style with pearls woven throughout.

She was like something too beautiful and perfect to touch. And yet touch her he would. The moment they were alone again.

You have duties here. You cannot afford to be endlessly distracted by your wife.

'You look beautiful,' he said.

Her lips curved slightly. 'And you look stunning,' she returned.

The words hit him with a strange force to his chest. He had not expected…compliments from his bride.

'Is that true?'

'I have always thought so. And I have wished to tell you so many times. When you were dressed to go out to a party… It almost hurt to look directly at you. Like the sun.'

'That is a level of flattery that I do not need,' he said, while at the same time it filled him with a sense of perverse pleasure.

'It is not flattery if it's true.'

They went out to the carriage, the staff moving in step to a perfect dance. Giving them their cloaks, opening doors, helping them inside. As if they had never been gone. As if Eleanor had always been the Duchess.

And then they set off for the rather short trip to Beatrice and Briggs's home.

'It's so strange,' she said. 'Coming back here. It was easier to take it all in when we were in Scotland.'

'How so?'

'I felt like a different person, so it did not seem so strange to be living an entirely different life. Here... I was your ward here. As I was back at Bybee House. Everyone here knows it. I know it. And I cannot quite reconcile what I was with what is true now.'

'It does not matter what you were. It matters what you are.'

'If you say so, Your Grace.'

Whenever she called him that it sent a surge of erotic need through him. And he was fairly certain that she was aware of that.

They arrived at the front of the penthouse, and the dance began again, as they were ushered into the town house. 'The Duke and Duchess await in the formal dining room, Your Graces,' the butler told them.

And they were led into the perfectly appointed room, where there was a veritable feast laid out on the table.

'Eleanor,' Beatrice said, jumping up from the chair and encircling his wife in a hug.

'Nice to see you too,' he said.

'I am pleased to see you, as well, of course,' Beatrice said, though the greeting she gave him was much more circumspect.

'As you can see,' he said. 'She has not come to any harm.'

'We will have to ask her to confirm that,' Beatrice said.

Eleanor blushed. 'I'm fine,' she said.

'You didn't have to kidnap her out of my home,' Briggs said.

'You did not lecture me via letter, why do you do it now?'

'Because the lecture is much more fun in person,' Briggs said. 'And anyway, I'm not going to get a hand cramp scolding you. But I'm happy to waste the words now that we are together again.'

'The security in your home is lax,' Hugh said. 'If I, not an experienced kidnapper, can make off with one of its occupants, then perhaps it is not me you should be upset with.'

'Touché,' Briggs said.

They all sat then, around the table.

'This is lovely,' Eleanor said, grinning, though he could see that she felt slightly strange.

'We do not stand on ceremony,' Briggs said. 'After all, why should we? We are all family now, in an official capacity, and of the same status. And have known each other for far too long.'

That seemed to relax Eleanor a great deal. 'I do not know what to do with the idea that we might be of the same rank,' she said. 'But I am relieved to not have to stand on ceremony, at least for another day.'

'Well. Given that tomorrow you'll be thrown to the wolves, it will be a nice reprieve.'

'Wolves?'

'Well,' Beatrice said. 'You've made a scandal.'

'Obviously,' Briggs said. 'The prevailing thought is that you have been seducing her this entire time. Doing God knows what in that country manor of yours. You are of course every bit the debauched figure that your father is, you simply hide it better. And you have thrown over a respectable woman for "a tart of your own making". Not my words, Hugh, don't punch me in the face.'

'Surely you must be exaggerating.'

'I am not. The only hope that either of you has is to come back looking like a happy couple. Staying away was not going to help. Especially given that the popular thought is that you have taken terrible advantage of her. They need to see that she is well. That she is happy.'

'I am happy,' Eleanor said.

'She's happy,' he said, feeling very much like he could not confirm that, but that he hoped it was true.

'He didn't have to marry me,' Eleanor said. 'That is what everyone is overlooking. You know he didn't have to. He could have made me a mistress. I'm not a lady. I was under his protection. He was the only person who would have called him out over his treatment of me. They are correct of course in assuming that he debauched me, there is no other reason that we would have flown off to Gretna Green. However…'

'I don't see why the debauchery needs to be a public discussion,' he said.

'Because you made it very clear,' Briggs said. 'Your impatience has revealed you.'

'You would think that it could make just as neat

an argument that I was not going to touch her until we could be wed.'

'We both know that isn't true, though. But that is not the point. The point is you will have an uphill battle gaining her acceptance. You will be fine. You are a duke, and no one will risk your ire. Neither will they risk mine. I have made it plain that I support you. But that doesn't change the fact that sympathies do not lie with you.'

'So everything that I have done, everything that I have built… It is ruined.'

'Yes,' Briggs said. 'You will have to build something new. Something entirely your own. Something entirely based on who you are now. Not what your father was, and not who you were before you went with Eleanor. That is your only hope.'

'Then it's good we returned. Because you are correct. The work must start now.'

After dinner, Eleanor and Beatrice took coffee in the Duchess's sitting room.

'I'm glad that you returned unscathed,' Beatrice said. 'I was beside myself when I realised that he had taken you from the house after we had refused to tell him where you were. We did not give you up.'

'I believe you. But I'm not unhappy. I ran from the prospect of a life as his mistress. I never thought that he would marry me.'

'You are happy.'

'We were very happy in Scotland. But there was no scandal there. And things were quite different. We

were able to just be ourselves for the first time in…
I like your brother. Very much.'

'I know that you do,' Beatrice said, grinning.

'No. You have known all the time that I fancied
myself in love with him. That I longed for him. That
I felt romantic towards him. But I like him as well.
And that was a new discovery upon this trip. We do
not have distance between us any more. I can… I
can speak with him. I don't have to bait him to get
an emotional reaction out of him. To incite his passion and… I'm sorry. You don't want to hear about
your brother's passion.'

Beatrice's smile turned slightly wobbly. 'Not especially. It is difficult, though, because you are my
very dear friend, and I care very much that you have
found the kind of happiness with him that I have with
Briggs. And passion is no small part of that.'

'Let me put your mind at ease by telling you that
passion is certainly no issue between the two of us.'

'I'm unsurprised. It has always been clear that it
was difficult for the two of you to withhold your-
selves from passion.'

'I never thought it was for him. But he wanted me.
As I have wanted him. And that…has changed everything. I desire him so much and I… I want more,
though. And I fear now that we're back here there
will only be less. He is a servant to his title, and he
must give more to society while we're here. Already
the entire conversation has centred around what we
might look like to other people. When we were in
Scotland none of that mattered. We did not have to

perform for anyone. We did not have to work to entertain them. We simply were. For the first time in my life… I have been able to rest in who I am. And what I want.'

'Well, that must change. Not now that you're back. You must be the Duchess that you are. Not the Duchess that Anna Paxton would've been. You are owed that. Your own moment. Your own version of what it is to be the Duchess.'

'But I'm nobody. I am not a lady. I am not titled. I'm not from this world.'

'You have lived in Hugh's world for a very long time, and you were a successful inhabitant of it. Do not allow anyone to make you feel like you are less. Least of all yourself. You belong here, because you are the one that he married. Never forget that. You are correct. He could have made you his mistress. He could've let you go. You were willing to go off and see yourself taken care of. You did not ask anything from him. He chose this. He chose you. Never let anyone make you doubt that.'

She felt bolstered by that. By the realisation. And she would take it, and use it as a shield against all that might come tomorrow.

Chapter Twenty

There was an intense sort of heaviness surrounding the preparation for the ball. She and her lady's maid agonised over which gown to select. It was important that they chose the right one. Important that she looked beautiful, but innocent, not like an ingénue or a debutante, but certainly not like a woman who had seduced away the man of a much more worthy lady, which was certainly the narrative that existed in the ballroom.

Hettie looked at her thoughtfully. 'I think the violet or the yellow suit you,' she said. 'You look lovely in those colours, and yellow often makes people look ill, but not you. You look the picture of spring in it, and also not like you possess any sort of wicked wiles.'

She laughed at that. 'Well. As it has already been decided that I must possess wicked wiles, perhaps it doesn't even matter.'

'It always matters. You can turn the tide, Your Grace.' Hettie looked positively giddy about using her title. But Eleanor had to wonder if it was related to the other woman's promotion that had come along with Eleanor's. But no. That wasn't a kind interpretation of Hettie, who had been a wonderful maid to her for all these years.

'I'm pleased that he finally saw what was in front of him the entire time,' she said. 'You obviously love him.'

Eleanor's cheeks went hot. 'Obviously?'

'I don't mean it in a bad way, miss. Your Grace,' she amended quickly. 'It's only that you clearly admire him so, and he is a fine man. A good man. A handsome man. Shouldn't he have a woman who sees him for all that he is? I'm glad that he chose you.'

'Maybe he didn't choose me. Maybe I simply seduced him with my feminine wiles.'

She laughed. 'That is the other problem. I know you. And you are good. And no one is more deserving of having such a boon as you. I don't believe you seduced him. But we all know what happened between the two of you that day.'

'Is the gossip in the house terrible?'

'Unlike those hens in the ballroom, we're taking your side. You have been nothing but respectable, and he… Well, in his attempt to maintain his snobbishness he let things get to a place between you where it was unbearable. He should never have got engaged to that woman. And we all know that. He never wanted her. That much was apparent.'

'Poor Lady Paxton,' Eleanor said. 'She did not ask for any of this.'

'No. She didn't. He on the other hand should have behaved better.'

'But for Hugh, he thought to maintain his dignity, his reputation. He wanted nothing more than to be perfect.'

'Being a duke doesn't make you perfect. Any more than not being a lady makes you less. Hopefully he understands that now.'

An intense heaviness gripped her heart. 'Maybe. But the challenge now will be to hold our heads high as we walked back into that den of vipers.'

'Just be you,' she said. 'But be you in the yellow dress. And look at him the way that you always do. There will be no doubt that the two of you love one another.'

That the two of you love one another.

Those words echoed in her chest as they made their way to the ball.

She looked *sweet*. Hettie had made sure of that. She had the same pearls woven into her hair as she had done for dinner the night before, but while the green had made her look slightly older and more sophisticated, the yellow emphasised her youth.

She looked fresh-faced and innocent, and it made her laugh given that she had never in her life been less innocent than she was today.

Her heart was threatening to climb out of her mouth as the carriage pulled up to the massive house, illuminated grandly by candles and gas lamps all around. The front of the house had a whole line of carriages, as guests flooded inside.

And when he took her arm this time, it was not in the proprietary fashion he had done so all the other times they had come to balls this season. No. This time, he took her arm as a husband would a wife.

And they stepped inside, all eyes turning to them. The crowd parted as they walked through the crowded entry and into the ballroom. 'The Duke and Duchess of Kendal,' came their introduction as they walked inside.

She could see Anna. It was as if there was an arrow drawn directly between them.

And guilt rose up inside her. She felt the need to speak to her. Felt the need to say something. To do something.

Anna turned away from her, and she could not blame her.

With sweaty hands, she kept her hold on Hugh's arm.

'Don't leave me,' she said.

'I won't,' he said, putting his hand over hers and looking at her in a way that seemed to suggest she was the only person in the room.

He was probably doing it for the benefit of everyone else that was there.

And why wouldn't he? This was what they were supposed to do. Look like a couple. A couple that was undeniable. A couple that could no more have stayed away from each other than stopped breathing.

They had to become a love story. But the problem was, for her they already were.

And she did not think it was the same for him.

He had wanted her, but he spoke of it with such regret. As if it was an illness, rather than desire.

She was not complaining. Not really. Because how could she? She had secured a marriage that would keep her safe, more secure than any other marriage could have. And he was... Him.

He had the first dance with her, and she could feel everyone watching them. It was the strangest thing. Usually, she felt one set of eyes on her out of all. His.

Now they were together, and they were drawing the stares of absolutely everyone.

When they finished with the first dance, she was thirsty. Still reluctant to leave his side, but she had determined that she needed to speak to Anna. 'I need to... I would like some punch,' she said.

'I will fetch some for you.'

'Thank you.'

She would slip away just for a moment while he attended to that task. She did not wish for him to come along when she spoke to Anna. She wanted to do it herself.

She did not know if it was wise. She didn't want to draw any more attention to Anna than was already on her, and she did not want the other woman to think that she was simply on a mission to repair her own reputation. That had nothing to do with it. If she was heartbroken...then she was heartbroken and Eleanor was as well. Because Eleanor had been prepared to watch Anna marry the man that Eleanor wanted. And she knew how badly it hurt. The fact that she had... She had won, she supposed, didn't make her feel triumphant. She was happy. Glad that Hugh had married her instead of Anna, but she felt no triumph over it.

She saw Anna slip out onto the balcony, and decided that she would meet her there. She picked through the crowd of people, and went through the door closest to her. And then much to her chagrin, found herself running into the Earl of Graystone.

'Oh,' she said.

He caught her elbow, and looked down at her, stunned for a moment, it seemed, as if he could not believe that it was her.

'You're back,' he said.

'Yes,' she said. 'We just arrived in London yesterday.'

He dropped her arm suddenly, taking a step back. 'We. You and your husband.'

'Yes,' she said.

'Did you mock me, the two of you? That I came to ask for your hand when the Duke was already screwing you?'

The words hit her like a fist. She was not innocent, but still, hearing it said like that...

Hugh used coarse language in the bedroom, but it was not the same thing. He did not use it to degrade her. It excited them both.

This was meant to crush her beneath the heel of this man's boot. Shame her.

And she refused.

'He was not,' she said. 'There is an affection that exists between the two of us, and always has. But he was never... The Duke was never inappropriate with me. And he never took advantage. We had feelings for each other that… That were impossible. And when it came down to it, neither of us could marry someone else.'

'That is a very nice story that the two of you concocted out in the wilds of Scotland. But we all know it isn't true. Not strictly.'

'I do not have to explain myself to you. I never made any promises to you, and it was the Duke who denied your offer. I do not regret it, not now. But as for my intentions… I thought that we would marry. However, given the way that you handle a disappointment, I can only say that I am glad that we did not make a match. It says much more about a man the way that he handles a loss than the way he handles a win.'

She turned to go and he grabbed her arm again, and she was surprised when a woman's voice broke between them. 'Sir, you must unhand the Duchess. You are making a fool of yourself. If your intent was to shame her, then it has backfired spectacularly, for I have witnessed the entire exchange from across the terrace, and the only person who is owed any measure of shame is you. Unhand her.'

'Why should you defend her?'

She turned and saw Anna standing there, her expression placid, almost serene. But there was an iron to her voice and to the set of her shoulders that told Eleanor she was not a woman to be trifled with.

'I know better than to foist blame for anything onto a woman when there is a duke involved,' Anna said. 'Unhand her and step away.'

The Earl looked at them both, his lip curled. 'Is his prick made of gold that the two of you forsake all sanity for him?'

'It is not about the quality of his character,' Anna said. 'But of mine. I will thank you to never again attempt to besmirch my honour. Now go off and try to collect what remains of yours. But I'm sad to inform you, that is very little.'

And he did leave then, with Anna's piercing gaze following after him.

Silence fell between them, and as she turned to walk away, Eleanor caught hold of her. 'I was coming out here to speak to you,' Eleanor said.

'Why is that, Eleanor?'

She did not use her title, and Eleanor supposed she was owed the slight. Especially given that she had just come to her rescue.

'I wanted to tell you how sorry I am. With the way things went. You deserved better. You deserve better. I also wanted you to know that I… I never intended for any of this.'

Anna looked resigned then sad. 'He wanted you from the beginning. I knew that I did not have his full attention. I was a fool for ignoring it. I was married once already. And I did not have my husband's love then either. But then, he did not have mine. With the Duke… I could see myself loving him. He's a fine man. A handsome man. A good man.'

She sounded wistful. For all that could have been.

'I'm very sorry…'

'My heart is not broken. I suspect that like him I

suffer greatly from the fact that someone else had my affection first. And I will never care for anyone else the way that I did for him.'

'Well why can't you be with that man?'

'Because he's dead, Eleanor.'

Eleanor recoiled slightly from the stark words. 'I thought you didn't love your husband.'

'It wasn't my husband. It was another man. And he was… He was part of the household when I was growing up. A servant. He was not for me. But that did not stop me from wanting him. I was married off very quickly because my father could see that I was…and the boy went away. And then he died. And he never knew that I… He never knew. I may not be able to love him in the way that I would wish. I may never be able to be with him, but I fear no man will ever have my heart as long as he does. So I cannot even be angry at the Duke for wanting you, and not being able to force himself to want another. I cannot be. I understand too well.'

'He doesn't love me,' Eleanor said.

'But you love him.'

She nodded, trying to swallow. 'I have… I always have. And what we are… It is impossible. It was. It should've been.'

'Some things cannot be denied. Unfortunately when you try to deny them there are usually other victims brought into the play.'

'Yes. And that is exactly what we have done to you.'

'It is what was done to my first husband. Thankfully, I did not have the ability to break his heart.'

'But I'm sorry. For any indignity that you've suffered because of us.'

'I'm not going to tell you that all is forgiven because I'm still dealing with everything. But had things gone differently, I think that we might've been friends, Eleanor. However, I was sadly prepared for the fact that you would be my rival in my marriage, and I suppose I should be thankful that it all happened now.'

'Had he married you, it would not have happened.'

Anna looked at her and shook her head sadly. 'Do you still not understand? If he had that kind of restraint where you were concerned, it would never have happened at all. It would have happened if we were married, the same as it did when we were engaged. And he would've made himself a liar and you an adulterer, and he as well. You would've both betrayed your vows for one another. I believe that firmly. All the better that you made them to each other. I cannot truly be angry with the way things worked out...'

'And perhaps it is not me or the Duke who had truly sinned against you,' Eleanor said, desperate to patch all of this up, to fix it. To make it nicer and better and not this spiky, terrible thing that made something so beautiful hurt quite a lot. 'I think perhaps that society is at fault. Is that not why you were not suited to the man you loved first? It's why he was trying desperately to find a marriage with someone else, anyone other than myself, and why he was looking for a husband for me as well. If it weren't for other people, we just could have been together.'

'I suppose you can make them your villain if you wish. But I've learned railing against society changes nothing. Not practically. We all must play by these rules, and so we are as we're made, here in this beautiful prison we cannot escape.'

Eleanor looked behind them, the windows to the ballroom glowing with gold light. This gilded cage…

She wondered if Hugh's cage was all the smaller, for all the more gold it had.

'Perhaps not. Thank you… Thank you for coming to my aid. It is more than many would've done.'

'One thing I cannot stand is a man who takes his weaknesses out on a woman. I'm far too familiar. And I would not allow him to do that to you. Above all else, Eleanor, I know who has the real power here. It is not you. And it is not me. Any more than it is the role. He is the one who has the most to answer for.'

'He…'

'There you are.'

She turned and saw her husband standing there, a glass of punch in his hand. 'I certainly did not expect to find you out here.'

'Your Grace,' Anna said.

And, unlike the Earl, Hugh kept Anna's eye contact. 'Lady Paxton.'

'You should take better care of your bride,' she said. 'She had an encounter with a serpent. But thankfully, she handled herself admirably. Be well,' Lady Paxton said, nodding before walking away.

'What happened?'

'The Earl of Graystone is a very sore loser. And I am thankful that you turned him away.'

'If only I had done it out of anything other than petty jealousy. I did not care for his gambling debts, it's true, but I did not truly have an issue with his character. I simply wanted what he was asking for.'

'Well. It was Lady Paxton who came to my rescue. She handled it commendably. There is no problem with her character. And I... I am sorry that I caused her any pain.'

'As am I.'

'She didn't love you.'

He looked at her and laughed. 'I did not think she did.'

'It just never occurred to you to marry a woman who actually loved you?'

'Not at all. It was never a consideration. I simply wanted someone who was suitable.'

'You don't think of love at all?'

He lifted a shoulder. 'My mother loved my father very much, by all accounts. And what good did it do her? He squandered that love. He did not deserve it. He broke her. Dealing with a sickly child as she was, and him bringing nannies into the household and playing with them. And my mother...just disappeared into herself. More and more with each passing year. With each passing day in the end. My father seemed to enjoy the fact that she loved him. He gave none of it in return, and he simply used it as a consolidation of his power against her. He so enjoyed those games. And she always wanted him. No matter what, she always wanted him.' He looked haunted by that. 'What a manipulation love is. I've never had any interest in it.'

Eleanor had known love. Her father had loved her mother. Her father had loved Missy. And he had loved her as well. His love had never been selfish. He had been a good man. A kind man. How would things have been for Hugh if his father had been different? If his father had been a much kinder man altogether?

'Well, then I suppose you should feel better being absolutely certain she didn't love you.'

'I do,' he said. 'The last thing I would ever have wanted was to hurt her in that fashion.'

But Eleanor didn't feel better. Because the truth was, she did love him.

And he had the power to hurt her in whatever fashion he chose.

The ball had been a success in terms of improving the view of their marriage somewhat. The next day they took a turn about Rossiter Square, making sure that they continued to look enchanted with one another.

He couldn't quite let go of the thought that he had made a misstep with her last night, for all that the take on the two of them as a married couple seemed to have improved amongst the *ton*. He was not entirely certain if he trusted anything. As he had now been told repeatedly his perspective as both a man and a duke disqualified him from seeing or understanding certain things.

It was a strange thing not to be able to trust the inherent authority of his own opinion, as he had done all of his life until now.

Last night, after the ball, it had been late. And they had gone to their separate rooms. He had not gone to her afterwards, and he was wondering now if he should have. He had felt that perhaps it was the courteous thing to leave her alone, but he wondered now if it was contributing to the subtle sense of separation between them. Not that they looked as if there was any separation between them. For all the world could see, they appeared perfectly in harmony. He had never appreciated what a good actress Eleanor was.

But then, he had to wonder if these past years the two of them had been engaging in some of the finest acting ever seen. They had played for themselves and for others that they did not desire one another. And that was truly a feat.

Things had felt easy in Scotland, though, and he had not questioned himself with her. But here…

Here he did. There was a part for both of them to play and he had to be a duke, first and foremost, and a man second.

With her in his home, in his bed, he was not quite sure how to accomplish it.

'We will finish the month here, and then return to Bybee House before the end of the Season.'

'We will?' she asked, looking up at him, her expression slightly stunned.

'Yes. That is only five more days.'

'I am aware when the end of the month is. I'm surprised you do not wish to finish the Season, that we might continue to build upon our reputation.'

'I have the feeling it would be best for us to return home and see to the running of the household. My obligations in the House of Lords will be finished in these next couple of days. There is no real reason to linger. I think there is something powerful in returning, putting on a bit of a show, and then going off to rusticate.'

'You would know more about these sorts of games.'

'It is not a game,' he said.

'It is,' she said.

'It is nothing more or less than my life, Eleanor. I have never known it to be any different. And I doubt we ever will. Being a duke requires a certain amount of public performance. It is something my father never engaged in. He did not see to his duties, he did not uphold any dignity or honour in connection with our name, he did not protect my mother. I will not do that. I will do what must be done.'

'How nice for you.'

'Do not be cross with me,' he said. 'I do this for you as well.'

'I know,' she said. 'It makes me miss Scotland a great deal.'

And he felt that. Agreed with that. But there was no point in saying so. So he said nothing. Simply manoeuvred the carriage they were driving in more slowly around the pond. When he was satisfied they had been seen, they returned to the town house.

And he began dealing with the obligations that he had to his position in government.

It kept him busy. The hunt for a wife had put some of this into the background, and now it must come to the fore so that he could finish everything before his departure.

They would attend one more ball, Eleanor would have several lunches.

And as they dealt with these commitments, they became like ships passing in the harbour, moving at different times. They found time to make love twice. He came to her room, and she gave herself to him joyfully, but afterwards, he went back to his own chamber, and he wondered if that was the right thing to do.

She never came to him. But then, that did not surprise him. She would be too timid to do that.

Five days on from that conversation, they packed all their items, and made an entire caravan of staff, for the trip back to Bybee House.

They stayed at a roadside inn on the way back, and he made love to her there as they had been in Scotland.

It felt better. Freer than anything had since coming back to England.

But they did not speak of it, though he held her through the night.

When they returned to Bybee House, she was subdued, her eyes wide as she looked at the place.

'What is it?' he asked.

'I cannot quite believe the change that has occurred since we left here.'

'It is… Unexpected.'

'Your mother knows, doesn't she?'

'Of course. I have sent her correspondence.'

'Did she respond?'

'No,' he said, his voice tight.

He had no idea what his mother's take would be on the whole thing. And he could not guess. She might be supportive. Particularly if she thought they had feelings for one another. But she might also be angry with him. It might remind her a bit too much of his father, and he could not blame her if it did.

They walked inside, and the look of trepidation on her face made him wish to fight every imaginary villain she saw before her.

The housekeeper stood at the base of the stairs, her expression carefully neutral, and he knew that whatever the staff thought, they would keep it to themselves. They had worked for the family long enough to do well at averting their eyes if there was scandal. His father had created vastly more scandal than this.

'Welcome home, Your Graces,' she said.

'Is my mother in her sitting room?'

'Yes,' she said, nodding.

'Thank you. You go upstairs,' he said to Eleanor. I will come and find you soon.'

But Eleanor did not budge.

'I would like to speak to your mother,' she said.

She had never once pushed back at his designated plan since they had married. In fact, their relationship had been much more harmonious than it was when he had been her guardian and she his ward. She seemed to respect the position of husband with much greater authority. But she was pushing back now.

'I do not know my mother's opinion on the union.'

'I have my own relationship with your mother. And I would like to be there when you speak to her.'

He could see that she would not budge on this matter, and if he wanted to avoid having an argument in front of his housekeeper, then he would have to oblige her.

'Come then,' he said.

She followed him through Bybee House and into the sitting room, where his mother sat, a cup of tea perched on the table beside her.

'You've come home,' she said.

'Yes, mother. I brought my wife as well.'

And she surprised him then. Because she smiled. 'I did not write you back because I could not quite believe it until I had seen it. You've done well,' she said.

And he felt Eleanor sag beside him in relief.

'I was not certain your opinion was favourable.'

'I like Lady Paxton very much. But Eleanor is already a daughter to me. And I am thankful that if I must surrender my home to another woman…it is to this one.'

'Mother…'

'Leave us,' she said. 'I wish to speak to my daughter.'

Eleanor felt completely stunned by the easy acceptance of the Dowager Duchess.

She had imagined a great many scenarios, but this was not one of them.

'Sit, dear girl. I will have tea brought for you.'

'You are not shocked?'

She shook her head. 'I have known that you admired my son for a very long time. I was sorry for you, because I know what it is to admire a man so greatly and have him not return the feeling.'

'Oh.' She was not sure how she felt that everyone had a concept of her feelings for Hugh. She had rather hoped that they were a bit more secretive than that. Though he hadn't known. Which was perhaps a testament to him more than it was anything else.

'Be very careful,' she said. 'You should never love a man so much that he has the power to break you.'

'He would…'

'I know my son. He is a good man. And he has worked very hard to overcome the shortcomings of his father and my own. But… He is also human. And I feared… Men, darling, they do not feel things the same way that we do. They can make love to another woman on a whim, and never think of it as a betrayal. It destroys us.'

She spoke with such conviction, and Eleanor knew that it came from a place of pain. Of experience. But still, she could not imagine…

'I am very glad that he married you. It is better. For both of you. You will make him happy.'

'How can I make him happy if you think he might still stray?'

'As I said. It is different for men. My darling, you

don't have a mother to give you advice. I am just telling you what I think you need to know to be kept safe.'

She thought of Missy. And how she had done the same. Warned her of men and their appetites. It seemed to her that she had been given a lot of warnings based on the nature of men as a whole.

Men in general.

But none of it had anything to do with Hugh. She had been so convinced that he would never marry her because of what Missy had told her. But in the end, he had. Because that was who he was. It was how he saw things. It went with his code of integrity. And on that very same note, she was certain that he would be a faithful husband. Even though things had not been quite the same between them since they had come back to England. They had, though, when they had stopped in the roadside inn.

That same inn where he had slept on the floor by the door. But this time he had joined her in bed, and his hands had been on her body, and it had been wonderful.

They cared for each other. If nothing else, there was that. And she did not think that he would hurt her. Not on purpose. Not ever.

'Thank you. I'm very glad that you approve of the marriage. I do care for him. Very much. And I will do everything that I can to give him the best life possible. To be worthy of the honour that he has given me. I understand that I am not of the same station.

And that I am not quite what you might have hoped your son would marry.'

'Given my own experiences with marriage, all I ever wanted for my children was for them to find a level of happiness that I could not. Your title, your station, it does not matter to me. Because a title and station will not protect you from disappointment. It will not protect you from a broken heart. I would rather you start at least with the building blocks of happiness. Something that I could never achieve regardless of the fact that I was much closer to my husband in social standing.'

'There is a bit of a scandal with our marriage.'

She shook her head. 'It was never the scandal that mattered. It was the hurt. Had he kept all of those things private, it would have been no better. In fact, it might've been worse. At least he was an embarrassment. At least all of England knew why my heart was broken. Better than suffering and having everyone wonder why the Duchess of Kendal could not smile.'

'I suppose so.'

She left the conversation feeling a range of emotions that she could not quite explain.

She felt guarded, but cautiously optimistic about what lay ahead. The acceptance of the former Duchess meant so much to her. That she thought she could make Hugh happy mattered.

But she painted a bleak picture of matrimony, and Eleanor simply couldn't fathom ever being in that position. She wanted to speak to Hugh, but he wasn't around, and when she inquired as to his whereabouts, she was told that he was off seeing to a tenant. They had been away, and now there was extra to be done.

She admired her husband's work ethic. She always had. But she felt a bit unhappy that it meant he did not have every moment of the day to spend with her. She waited for him all day, and he did not return. And finally, she decided that it would be best to wait for him in the only room he would certainly appear in.

His bedchamber. And perhaps that was a wholly inappropriate thing to do even as his wife. But she missed him. And she did not like sleeping in separate rooms. It was difficult and strange to be apart. But she didn't know if he shared the same feelings.

You could ask.

That was the problem. She was beginning to think she would have to ask something she didn't want to ask. Give him opinions that she had been holding back. It was easy to fall into the idea that she should be so grateful for the union that she had no right to ask for anything.

But this was her life. The life that she was going to live with him from here on. And maybe she could. Maybe she could ask for what she wanted. Maybe she could tell him.

When he came in, he looked exhausted. His face was streaked with dirt, his jacket was off, the sleeves of his shirt pushed up past his elbows. He looked... He was the most beautiful thing she had ever seen.

'What happened?'

'There was an issue with some cows out in the field. I stopped to help.'

'Oh...'

'I didn't expect to find you here. I rather expected my valet.'

'Just me. I'm sorry.'

His gaze turned hungry, and seeing that hunger was a relief. 'You misunderstand me. I'm not disappointed.'

'I would like to draw you a bath.'

'You don't need to do that,' he said.

'No. I want to. And I know how to do it. One of the perks of having a wife who is not a lady.'

'Why don't we have the servants assist?'

She rang for his valet, who commissioned the tub to be filled with steaming water.

And then they were left to their own devices. She began to help him out of his clothes, and admired every hard, honed inch of him as he stepped into the water. And then she began to take off her own clothes.

He growled in appreciation as she stripped herself of her dress and stood before him completely naked.

It was amazing how easy it was to stand before him like this. As if her body was always meant for this. To be seen by him. Admired by him. Touched by him. And she felt equally that his body was made for hers.

For her enjoyment. Her appreciation. Hers and hers alone.

'I want you to promise me,' she said, stepping into the tub, putting her knees on either side of his thighs and moving towards him. 'That there will never be any other woman. Only me.'

'Did we not already discuss this? Wife. Mistress. Ward.'

'Yes. But I wish you to say it again. Your mother has low confidence in the ability of men to remain faithful. But I will not share my husband.'

'And I will not share my wife. Nor will I share myself with anyone else. It is only you, Eleanor. I promise you that.'

'Good. I will give you whatever you wish. We can... We can share a room. That way I'm always there when you want me. When you need me.'

He looked up at her, his expression filled with something like wonder.

'If you wish.'

'I do.'

'The servants may talk. It is very unfashionable for a husband and wife to share a room.'

'I hope they do talk. If I don't share your room, am I not just the same Eleanor that I was before we left?'

'You were not the same. And you never will be. You are my wife now.'

'Or maybe it's just that I was never what I thought I was. Everyone seems to know... Everyone seems to know that I wanted you well before I thought anyone did. It is humbling, to realise that I kept my secret so poorly.'

'I didn't know.'

'Do you know now,' she asked, arching her hips forward so that she brought the heart of her close to his thick shaft.

She felt his body lurch beneath the water, and

groaned when he came into contact with that part of her that longed for him most of all.

But she denied them both, tilting her head back slightly, putting some distance between them as she took a cloth and began to scrub it over his chest.

He groaned. 'This is quite the tease.'

'I think you're up to the challenge. You are a man of such great restraint.'

'I was. Once. But you have tested that. No, you have more than tested that. You have shattered it.'

'I don't mind being the cause of such a reckoning. Perhaps it is good for you. Perhaps it is good for us. We have to reckon with what we believed about the world. What we believed about ourselves. I don't want the marriage that your parents had.'

'You know me well enough to know that I want nothing to do with how my father was. I want nothing in my life to mirror his.'

'When I spoke to your mother this afternoon, I could only think… I could only think that I would not sit quietly by living a life that I did not wish to live. It is important to me. That I can have honesty with you. I… I am so grateful for everything that you've done for me. But I cannot live a life only in gratitude.'

'No, but I didn't expect you to. I have never thought that I did you a favour, Eleanor. Make no mistake of that. I am quite realistic about my feelings. As a man. In every way. Being married to me is not the gift that others might've been tempted to believe that it is.'

'Why not?'

'I will always, first and for ever, be dedicated to

my title. That is simply the way of it. I will not be like
my father. I will not put my pleasure or my pursuits
of pleasure above these things.'

That made her feel sad. She wanted… She wanted
to be the most important thing to him. And it was
churlish and unfair of her to think that. Especially
since she had never once thought of a life where she
might have love, all she had ever thought of was security.

But the fact was, she loved him. Whatever she tried
to tell herself, whatever she imagined, she loved him.

'But you will always be first for me,' she said.

He looked up at her, and touched her cheek.

'Will I?'

'I'm your helpmeet. I am everything, and anything
that you need me to be. I'm yours.'

'And how do you find the strength to offer such
a thing?'

'It is much simpler than you might imagine.'

It was because she loved him, but the words stuck
in her throat. She didn't want to say them, she wanted
to protect herself. It was too difficult to admit such
a thing. She loved him.

But she buried that, and instead she leaned forward and kissed him. He reached up, his hand tight
in her hair.

'What I do want you to promise me, is that we
don't lose this,' she whispered against his mouth. 'It
was different when we were in London. Measured.
And I don't want measured. I want everything. By
day, perhaps it is your title that has your full alle-

giance, but by night, can I not have all of you? Give
me all your desire. All your need. Give me everything.'

He tugged her hair harder, drawing her head back,
and kissing her throat. And she moaned, wriggling
against him, desperately seeking more of what he
might offer.

'Hugh,' she moaned.

'It is difficult,' he said. 'To be like this with you.
To be like this with you in these places. I always separated these things. I've considered it a weakness,
always.'

'This is not a weakness,' she said, bringing the
heart of herself more firmly against the source of his
arousal. 'This is our strength. This is what made it so
we could no longer deny each other. This is why we
are together. How is that a weakness? It might have
been, if we had met other people. Anna said… She
said that she was certain both of us would've violated
our marriage vows to be with one another eventually.
She said she did not think we would ever have been
able to stay away from each other, and I think that
might be true. That we are as inevitable as the sun setting and the moon rising. As stars in the sky. Perhaps
we are meant to be. And perhaps you haven't decided
that you were always meant to be mine. I know that
I was always meant to be yours. And we do not have
to be separated. For I am here. I'm not at a brothel
in London, I am in your home, and I will share your
bed. I am the one who created this desire inside of
you, and I am the one who can satisfy it. Let me.'

They were beautiful words. A different sort of vow. Not the ones that had been spoken over an anvil in haste, but the ones that had been created inside her for just this moment.

They were halves to a whole. They were what each other needed. Deeply and certainly. One hand still in her hair, he wrapped his arm around her waist like an iron vice, and pulled her down onto him so that she could rub herself against his desire.

She moaned, panting with her need. She was slick and ready with her arousal, and she desired him more than she desired her next breath.

She loved it. Their skin wet and warm, their need unsatiated, as they had not had time to explore each other as they had done during their honeymoon. This was different.

They were different.

He was the Duke, and she the Duchess, in their home, and still, they had this. This great, unrelenting need.

She found herself being lifted out of the water, and then he brought her back down over his face, looking at her with an intensity that nearly made her scream. She gripped the edge of the tub, bracing herself on it as he held onto her, devouring her like beast.

She let her head fall back, panting, grateful for his strength, without which she would surely fall.

He licked her until her climax rocked her. And then he continued. He loved listening to her beg.

And then, after she had climaxed again, and again,

he lowered her against his body, when she was bone-
less and restless and spent.

He manoeuvred her to the bed, walking her in
front of him, and bent her over the mattress. He positioned himself behind her, and thrust into her in
one hard stroke. This was primal, basic. An intense
meeting of bodies, and yet she knew that their spir-
its met as well.

He gripped her so hard she knew that he would
leave bruises, and she would admire each and every
one. A testament to the truth that this thing between
them was no longer fantasy, but reality.

That he was hers. And she was his.

And she was glad of it.

And when he poured himself into her, it was on
a shout, his body pulsing inside her, and she luxuri-
ated in the feeling.

'Everyone knows,' he said. 'Everyone knows exactly what we're doing.'

'Good,' she whispered. And she meant it.

And what she didn't say, still, was that she loved
him. Because she was afraid of what would happen
when she finally did speak those words, and she got
nothing but silence back.

Chapter Twenty-One

True to his word, he was the Duke by day, and he was all hers at night.

He had moved her into his bedchamber, and he was extremely happy with the decision. He hadn't realised that having a wife could be quite so...

Was it because she was a wife, or because she was Eleanor?

He ignored the question that he asked of himself and brought his axe down onto a piece of wood, splitting it and sending the pieces flying hither and thither.

It was good to get out and do physical labour. All the time in London had felt stagnant, and the time and Scotland had been distinctly separate from reality. An entirely different sort of situation from what he was used to.

He didn't have as much time to spend with Eleanor during the day as he might like. But she seemed to keep herself busy running the household, planning the menu. She was graciously sharing some of that with his mother, and while that would normally not be the way it all worked, Eleanor insisted that it was fine with her, and that it was different, since his mother had had a hand in taking care of her for most of her life when she had been his ward.

He was glad that his mother had a companion that she loved so much.

They were settling in. They had found something that worked. A change that pleased all involved.

And he should be glad of that, but he could feel something... Something unsettled.

Sometimes he could feel reticence from her. Quiet.

And usually, they were both happy to overwhelm it with a physical storm. The passion between them was so strong, and it was easy to take refuge in that, so he did.

Being with her in that way.

He thought of her now, the way that she often rolled over in bed and straddled him, how she slept naked, which felt wanton and glorious. To be a man who had married a woman who wanted him in such a way...

He thought of what she said. That his passion had been created to match hers. That it was for each other. It was such a stunning thought. That perhaps he was insatiable, rough, because it was what she liked, and it had always existed inside of him to please her.

There was no one around, but still, he felt humiliated that he was standing out there getting aroused like a teenage boy while staring down at a piece of split wood.

Suddenly, he heard the sound of horse's hooves,

and he looked up, just in time to see Eleanor, riding on the back of a horse, as they had done in Scotland. But she was not filled with joy. Instead, she looked terrified.

The horse was spooked by something, and it was careening through the landscape at a dangerous clip.

There was a rock wall ahead, and the horse did not care that it was headed straight for it. Terror lurched through him, and he took off at a run, knowing that he was never going to catch a spooked horse. But he began to make noise, trying to divert the animal from its path.

It came to the rock wall, and balked, rearing up on its hind legs, and sending Eleanor off the back.

The sound that came out of him wasn't human.

He ran across the space with his heart threatening to burst in his chest.

'Eleanor,' he shouted.

She was unconscious, lying on the ground, and the first thing he thought was that she had broken her beautiful neck. And he would never... He would never be able to go on. He would never be able to...

The terror that seized him was so great that he was nearly sick with it, but he didn't have time to be sick. He had to take care of Eleanor. He put his hands on either side of her neck, felt that it was still intact. Felt her pulse beating there at the base of her throat, and nearly cast up his accounts. He picked her up, leaving the horse, running back to the estate as quickly as possible. One of the groundskeepers saw him.

'Your Grace?'

'Fetch a physician,' he shouted. 'Now.'

'Yes, Your Grace,' the man said, taking off at a run, while Hugh continued to the house.

'I need warm cloth. And a cold cloth. Whatever you have.'

The household staff began to clamour around him, especially when they saw that he was carrying the unconscious Duchess.

His mother appeared from the drawing room. 'What happened?'

'She's fallen off the horse. And she isn't awake.'

'Oh,' his mother said, her hand to her chest. She sat down, her face pale.

And it reminded him far too much of when Beatrice was ill. When her breathing was wrong, when they had to get the doctors. When they didn't know if she would last the night. This was all far too familiar. Far, far too familiar. Eleanor was his to protect. His wife, his mistress, his ward. Everything. And she was in this position... How many had failed to protect her?

How had he failed?

He took her upstairs and set her in the bed, sitting on the edge and touching her cheek, patting it lightly. 'Eleanor,' he said. 'Eleanor.' Each time he said her name he became more and more insistent, and yet still, she didn't stir.

'Eleanor,' he said gruffly.

Something built inside his midsection, a sound that was not human. He did not know it. He did not recognise himself.

He was a man who controlled everything. Absolutely everything, and he could not make his wife wake up.

Had she hit her head that hard?

Would she ever awaken? He recalled seeing the pallor in his father's face before he had slipped off into death.

His father had deserved death. Eleanor didn't deserve to die. She did not have that colouring to her face. She still looked so alive. She had to live.

It was only a few moments later when the doctor burst in. It was an echo of all the times Beatrice had been ill, down to the identity of the doctor. 'Your Grace. Tell me what happened.'

'She was on the back of a horse, and she fell. He spooked.'

He opened her eyes, moving a candle back and forth in front of them and examined them. 'I suspect she hit her head.'

'I know that, you idiot,' he said. 'Anyone can see that. It is apparent. Why won't she wake?'

'If there is an injury to the brain, or a bleed, she may not.'

'Do something.'

'There is little to be done with these sorts of things. We can give her laudanum if she is uncomfortable, but there is little else.'

He practically growled, putting his body between him and the door. 'Mend my wife.'

'Your Grace…'

'All those years with Beatrice. Bleeding her and feeding her laudanum. And she would have been better off on her own. Perhaps you don't know anything. The doctors in London say she can have a child.'

'Your Grace... I am an extremely cautious man. I've cared for your sister since she was a girl, and I would hate to see anything dangerous befall her. That is where my advice comes from. But it is not your sister that I'm here for now, it is your wife.'

'But what you are saying is unacceptable! I can do nothing but wait? Wait and see if my wife will die? You do not have a...a surgeon's trick or a medication to wake her? You have nothing?'

'Stay with her,' he said. 'Or have one of the servants stay with her. All night. Make sure that she does not stop breathing in her sleep. If so, you'll have to jostle her as best you can.'

'I will stay with her.'

'You have only to fetch me if you need me. When she wakes, fetch me.'

'And if she does not?'

'Then we must accept the possibility of bringing in a surgeon.'

He was despondent, sitting over Eleanor, keeping watch on her. And then at three hours past midnight, she stirred. Made a sound.

'Thank God,' he said to no one. No one but God himself. An entity he hadn't even thought to curse much less think of, until now.

Until now. 'Hugh,' she said.

'Eleanor,' he said. 'Eleanor.'

'Hugh,' she whispered.

She snuggled up against his chest, and he held her

there. And he knew that he needed someone to get the doctor, but he couldn't move. He could only hold her.

They lay like that for perhaps more than an hour before he fetched someone to go and get the physician, who came directly, and began to issue questions to Eleanor, who did not remember anything leading up to the accident.

'I just remember deciding to go riding,' she said.

'You're not an experienced enough horsewoman to be taking out an animal like that,' he said.

'I've been practising,' she said. 'I don't have enough to do during the day. And I've always wanted to ride. So I've been improving. But there was a snake on the footpath and…'

'I shall have it killed.'

'You don't need to have a snake killed. I have…' She winced.

'What's wrong?'

'My head hurts in a fearsome fashion.' She lay on the pillow, suddenly very pale. 'It is quite terrible.'

'I'm sorry,' he said, cradling her face. 'I'm sorry.'

And even though she made a fairly speedy recovery after that, things felt different. He could not bring himself to touch her at night, because he kept seeing her lying there, inert and unconscious. He could only see someone fragile. Breakable.

And it ate at him. He busied himself as best he could, did not come to bed until he had exhausted himself. His own arousal was a beast inside of him that he could not tame, but it was at odds with this feeling of terror that he felt every time he even considered taking her in his arms.

He was…undone by all of this. Everything had seemed clear before Eleanor. Everything. And then in Scotland he'd let himself believe it would work.

In London, it had been clear that he did not know how to balance being a duke and performing for society while contending with what she made him feel.

And then the accident…

He could not afford to be this way.

He had to have an heir. He knew that. But if she was pregnant, then that was a further risk to her health, and he would have to watch her endure that. And childbirth.

She knew that he was avoiding him, and he had the sense that he could not evade a conversation with her for much longer. Because that was how Eleanor was.

He wondered how different his life would be, how different his marriage would be, if he had not wed a woman who knew him quite so well. But the problem was, she did. And she was willing to speak to him in a way most women would never be willing to speak to a duke.

But she was not most women. She was Eleanor. She was different. She always had been.

'Your Grace…'

'It is out of deference to your recovery,' he said, not looking up from his paperwork that night when she came into his study.

'How did you know what I was going talk to you about?'

'Because I know you. And I have felt the change between us. But you were quite badly injured. And...'

'I'm not injured any more.'

'I thought you were dead,' he said.

'But I wasn't.'

'I am aware of that.'

'Did it frighten you so much?'

It had. It was near physical pain to admit to such a thing. But it had.

'I've seen people in a vulnerable state far too often.'

'Yes. And Beatrice was your responsibility, all through her childhood.'

'You have any idea what it's like to wait... To know that you can do nothing. I am a powerful man, as you are also quick to remind me, but I do not control life and death, Eleanor. It does not matter how much I wish for someone to keep on breathing. I am not in control of their health. I cannot make you wake up.'

And suddenly, her face went soft, and she did something unexpected. She cried. Tears began to roll down her cheeks, and she crossed the room to him and wrapped her arms around him. 'You have carried so much,' she said. 'So much.'

'Eleanor...'

'I want to take care of you, and instead I frightened you. I'm so sorry that I put all of that on you, after everything you've been through.'

'Do not treat me like I'm a child.'

'I'm not treating you like a child. I'm treating you like a man that I love. I do. I love you. So much. Very much. I love you more than I can explain. I have for years. You are… You are everything to me. You are my whole heart. I have never been able to explain it before. But it was as though from the first moment I saw you I knew that you were the single most important thing in my world. I thought at first it was because you were a duke and I was your ward. Because my association with you would determine my fate. Because the sort of match you could make me would determine my fate. But as I got older I realised it was different. I didn't simply admire you. I wanted you. I didn't simply want you. I loved you. And that day at the town house when you turned down the Earl of Graystone's proposal on my behalf, I decided that I would be your mistress, if that was the only way that I could have you. Because I loved you.'

'You loved me?'

'I do still,' she said.

The words felt like a knife had been taken and plunged directly into his chest, square into his heart.

Love.

What had love ever been but an enormous, untenable burden. Another person to love. Another person to care for. And following her there would be children. And what if one of them was like Beatrice? And what if…

All of it felt like too much. Far too much to bear. How could he be the best Duke, how could he be all the things that he needed to be while suffering beneath the burden of love? It was heaviness. It was sick rooms and his mother weeping in the corner. It was him trying to hold it all together while his father went out and did God knows what. It was nothing that he wanted. Nothing.

'Eleanor,' he said. 'I'm a duke above all else. And it cannot be that sort of marriage.'

'I just said that I loved you... I didn't ask you for anything in return.'

He thought of these past few days. Of the terror that he had lived with. Of the way that it had coloured everything he did.

He had not been able to think straight. What was she saying, she wasn't asking anything of him? She was asking everything of him. Whether she knew it or not. She was asking him for everything.

'Eleanor, it is impossible to...'

'We are not impossible,' she said. 'We are the only possibility. It was always going to be you and me, even if we broke everything to be together. Thankfully we only had to break a little bit. But don't run away now. I know... I know it's a lot. I know it...it's everything, Hugh. We are everything.'

'Eleanor...'

'I never wanted anyone but you. I tried. I tried. But it could never... I love you. Not because of what you could do for me. I would've taken nothing but you. The only thing that made me run away that day was the knowledge that I would have to share you with another woman. How small is that, how petty? I would've taken being ostracised by all of society to be your mistress, it was simply knowing that you would touch her and then touch me. I never needed your title. I never needed any of this. I never needed you to be perfect, and I never needed you to be a duke. All I ever needed you to be was you, Hugh. Does anyone else feel that way about you? Have they ever?'

He knew they had not.

Everyone else needed status. Needed his money. Needed protection. Even when they cared for him, that was the case. The only person it wasn't true of was Briggs, and it was because he already had everything that Hugh did.

Everyone else… Everyone else was beholden to him, beneath him. And this woman most of all. She had been his ward. And yet she was standing there offering something no one else ever had.

He knew how to be a duke. In Scotland he'd found out who he was as a man, not just the discovery of desire like he'd engaged in as a youth in brothels, but a real sense of who he was.

In London, he was forced to become both.

Eleanor was demanding he be both.

He did not know how.

It demanded he drop the shield he held in front of himself and it was an unfathomable request.

'I have work to do,' he said.

'Don't do that…'

'I have work that takes me to London. I shall leave tomorrow morning. Early.'

He needed to think. He needed to get away.

'And you will start rumours.'

'The rumours have started already. It was a mistake. All of this.'

'I'm your wife. You will not divorce me,' she said.

'Of course I will not,' he said. 'The scandal would be untenable.'

'Scandal. That is all you care about?'

'No,' he said.

'What else do you care about?'

'I need to go,' he said.

'I just love you. Why is that so terrible?'

'Because it is,' he said. 'And I cannot explain it any more than that. Because it is.'

He was the one to leave then, because she could not. And early the next morning he outfitted his horse and went away.

Chapter Twenty-Two

She was miserable. They were married, they would stay married. But she was miserable.

He didn't love her. And she had been expecting that. But what she hadn't expected was his rejection of the way she felt for him. It seemed so unfair. It seemed so particularly cold. Why could he not feel what she did. Why was it so unendurable for him to have her love? When he could have her body.

She knew that it had something to do with the accident. She knew that it did.

It had frightened him, she understood that, and she assumed it had something to do with Beatrice, but he wasn't sharing with her, so how could she truly know?

And when she missed her courses, she was shocked. Because after her accident, she had thought that if there was any hope she had been carrying a child, certainly it was lost after that.

But they still didn't come, and she knew that she needed to send word to him.

But she thought of her mother-in-law, and what she had endured. She had endured the indignity of her husband.

And Eleanor would not endure. She simply refused.

She asked that a carriage be outfitted for her.

'Does His Grace know you're coming to London?' Hettie asked.

'No. I don't intend to give him any forewarning. For it is not any of his concern.'

'Good for you,' her maid said quietly.

'You must come with me to London,' Eleanor said. 'Because I will be staying there for as long as it takes.'

They rode in the carriage together, with Eleanor in that claret-coloured gown that he loved so much. She did not look like an innocent designed to woo this time. Rather she looked like a seductress. And if she had to seduce her husband, then she would. If that was the only way to get him to accept her, to get him to take her love, then so be it.

She would do whatever it took.

Hugh had not slept well since he had left Bybee House.

His mother had sent him a terse missive in the time he'd been gone, but he had not responded. He didn't have to explain himself to his mother. He didn't have to explain himself to anyone.

He had been avoiding Briggs and Beatrice for that very reason.

Eleanor.

He did his best not to think of her. Not to think of anything.

He didn't have anyone that he spoke to about these things. The closest he had ever come to sharing his feelings with anyone was with Eleanor.

But how did you explain the way that the word love made you feel when it was like having the skin peeled from your bones? How did you explain the fear that came along with care? The burden that went with all of this?

There was no way to explain it.

He was sitting in his study when he heard a flurry of movement in the house.

And then the door to his study opened.

'The Duchess of Kendal has arrived,' the servant announced briskly.

'Has she?' he asked, his heart lifting slightly.

'Shall I…?'

'There is no need,' Eleanor said, sweeping into the room in a flurry of scarlet. 'I'm here. Thank you.' She turned and looked at the servant. 'You may close the door.'

The servant obeyed, leaving him closed in his study with the resplendent Eleanor who was drafted from the very depths of his fantasies.

'What are you doing here?'

'What I should've done a long time ago. I came to tell you that this is foolish. And it must be finished. We must not be at odds like this. Not any more. We must be together, Hugh, because we have been through too much not to be happy.'

'Eleanor…'

'I'm carrying it. I will carry it. The love that we have. You're not alone in this. I want to take care of you. I want to give to you. I will sit by your bed when you're ill, and I will hold your hand. I will pray for your help, and I will comfort you when our child is ill. When we are afraid, you can draw strength from me.'

He looked up at her, incredulous. 'And what if something happens to you? Who will comfort me then? Eleanor, I…'

The words got caught in his throat. 'Eleanor, all that I am has meant carrying this. All of it. And I have done so happily. But you… The world might rest on me, but all that I am rests on you. If I lose you…'

And it just all seemed impossible. So impossible that he couldn't breathe past it.

'What has you so afraid of this?'

'You don't know what it was like. To watch Beatrice cling to life year after year. To wonder if she would survive. Everyone thinks that I am an ogre, but they don't understand. They don't understand.'

'Of course they don't. No one except you could. You're the only one that has ever experienced what you have with her.'

'I…'

'She survived, Hugh. Against all odds. Rather than thinking of when she was sick, can't you be amazed that she is well? Isn't it an incredible thing? Isn't it?'

'You still don't understand…'

'I'm trying. I'm trying to…'

'You know what's worse than loving your dying

sister? Loving the man who is doing nothing to help. Loving the man who does nothing but break everything. It is a burden, Eleanor. Love is a burden, and it is indiscriminate. The fact that you love me does not mean I'm worthy of anything. For I loved my father until the day we buried him in the ground, and only then did I begin to separate myself from this agony. Only then. It has been hell. It has always been hell. It has only ever been hell.'

'Hugh, you're not a monster for loving your father. He is the monster for not valuing the family that he had. What he did to you, that was the monstrous thing.'

'I loved him all those years, and he gave me nothing. Nothing but more burdens to hold. And even now I'm trying to redeem him. Not about the name, it's about him. It…'

'We cannot live our lives for him any more. It is no different from the way we were living for society. We must live for us. And all those things that have come before, they do not get to decide what we are now. Must you be honourable at the cost of your happiness? Must you be safe at the cost of your joy? Why can we not simply be together. I love you. And if you cannot see a way to loving me…'

'I do,' he said, his voice rough, the words like a knife coming up through his throat, cutting him on the way out. 'I love you so much more than I have ever loved anything, and I find the prospect of it all terrifying. I am so afraid of what this need will do to me.'

'Because you've never seen love give you anything. But what if you trusted me. What if you trust me to replace all that loving me takes. And I trusted you to do the same. What if then we were left with so much joy we couldn't even contain?'

It seemed impossible. This thing that she was saying. But months ago they would've seemed impossible. She was the stars. Out of reach. And here she was now, wearing red, and right where he could touch her.

His other half. That piece of him that mattered so much.

And it didn't seem possible that happiness was standing right there, and all he had to do was reach out and take it. Hold it in his arms. No, it didn't seem possible. But what if it was.

Beatrice had found happiness, that was true. Beatrice was safe, and she was loved.

He had held it all, shielded everyone. He had done his best to not be his father. But maybe Eleanor was right. It wasn't enough to simply not be his father. He had to be himself.

He could no longer do things for that old man. Either to make up for him, or to try and redeem him. He could no longer hold onto those feelings.

He could no longer punish himself for what he felt, for what he didn't feel.

She was here. She was with him now. And she was offering a love, a life that was better than anything he could've ever imagined.

'I love you,' he said.

And she closed the space between them and threw her arms around his neck, kissing him. And he kissed her back, with all the love and feeling and ferocity that had been building up inside him for these days away from her.

'I have been a duke first my entire life. I wonder what would happen if I just loved you first and let everything else follow on after that.'

'Yes,' she whispered, smiling up at him. 'Do that.'

It felt so easy. And so hard all at once. But he was ready. She had been there all this time. Since that day she had looked up at him with that birthday cake in her hands, offering him the kind of love no one else ever had. And he had fought it all the way. Thinking he was resisting because of reputation. Because of society. But it had always only been to protect himself.

But it wasn't a life. Not one that he wanted. Not any more.

He would rather have Eleanor. And damn all the rest.

'I love you,' he said roughly.

'I love you too. I have something else to tell you.'

'What's that, my love?'

'I haven't had my courses this month.'

'Really?' And he was suddenly overcome with terror and joy in equal measure. 'A child...'

'Yes. Your child. And another chance to love. As yourself. Not anyone else.'

And he felt free then. For the first time in all his years, he felt free.

He was not a duke in that moment. He was just a man. Looking down at the woman he intended to spend the whole of his life with.

'I did not know when I agreed to be your guardian that you would end up taking care of me.'

'That makes me your wife, your ward, your mistress and your guardian. And that makes you my Duke, my husband, my lover.'

'You forgot one.'

'What's that?'

'You are also the love of my life.'

Epilogue

It could not be said that he was a calm father to be in the months that followed. He worried over every single twinge that Eleanor felt, and if it weren't so sweet, she might've been irritated with him by the end of it.

As it was, she couldn't be irritated with him at the end of it, because she was so consumed with the pain of labour.

But it was all worth it. Because his son, their son, was the most beautiful creature she had ever laid eyes on.

And as she watched Hugh holding their tiny baby, she still couldn't believe that not even a year ago he had been an impossible fantasy. And now he was her husband. And they had a child.

And the love between them burned brighter than anything she had ever known to dream.

'I have a son,' he said, his voice rough.

'I know that you could never fix things with your father. But you will make things right with him.'

He smiled. 'Love changes everything. I had not realised. I had not realised what it could change to simply love. Not to prove yourself worthy, but simply because you cannot help yourself.'

'I've never been able to help myself with you.'

'Nor I you. You are everything to me. Our home. Our family… It is everything to me. And whether we are scandalous or not outside these walls it doesn't matter. Because of all the love in them.'

One thing Eleanor had known for certain about Hugh Ashforth, the Duke of Kendal, was that he would not tolerate a scandal. But not only had he tolerated the scandal they'd created, he'd compounded it. Made it worse. Made it better. Let it go.

Because scandal didn't matter, not in the face of love.

With a love like theirs, nothing else mattered at all.

* * * * *

If you enjoyed this story,
be sure to read the other books in
Millie Adams's
Scandalous Society Brides miniseries

Marriage Deal with the Devilish Duke
Claimed for the Highlander's Revenge